the boy i love

also by nina de gramont

every little thing in the world

meet me at the river

the boy i love

nina de gramont

A
atheneum   *Atheneum Books for Young Readers*
New York   London   Toronto   Sydney   New Delhi

atheneum

ATHENEUM BOOKS FOR YOUNG READERS

An imprint of Simon & Schuster Children's Publishing Division

1230 Avenue of the Americas, New York, New York 10020

This book is a work of fiction. Any references to historical events, real people, or

real places are used fictitiously. Other names, characters, places, and events are products

of the author's imagination, and any resemblance to actual events or places

or persons, living or dead, is entirely coincidental.

Text copyright © 2014 by Nina de Gramont

Jacket photographs copyright © 2014 by Jill Wachter

All rights reserved, including the right of reproduction in whole or in part in any form.

ATHENEUM BOOKS FOR YOUNG READERS is a registered trademark of Simon & Schuster, Inc.

Atheneum logo is a trademark of Simon & Schuster, Inc.

For information about special discounts for bulk purchases, please contact Simon & Schuster

Special Sales at 1-866-506-1949 or business@simonandschuster.com.

The Simon & Schuster Speakers Bureau can bring authors to your live event.

For more information or to book an event, contact the Simon & Schuster Speakers Bureau

at 1-866-248-3049 or visit our website at www.simonspeakers.com.

Book design by Michael McCartney

The text for this book is set in Adobe Caslon Pro.

Manufactured in the United States of America

First Edition

2 4 6 8 10 9 7 5 3 1

Library of Congress Cataloging-in-Publication Data

Gramont, Nina de.

The boy I love / Nina de Gramont. — First edition.

pages cm

Summary: "Sixteen-year-old Wren has fallen in love with the most sought-after boy in school,

but his secret will both bring them together, and keep them apart."—Provided by publisher.

ISBN 978-1-4424-8056-8 (hardcover) — ISBN 978-1-4424-8058-2 (eBook)

[1. Love—Fiction. 2. Friendship—Fiction. 3. Secrets—Fiction.

4. Sexual orientation—Fiction.] I. Title.

PZ7.G76564Bo 2014

[Fic]—dc23

2013045455

For Hadley

Acknowledgments

Thanks to Peter Steinberg, world's best literary agent and longtime champion, and to Caitlyn Dlouhy for her continued belief in me, and her dedication to bringing out the best in my story and characters. Early readers Danae Woodward and Garrard Conley helped and encouraged. Thanks to Jessica Sit and everyone at Atheneum for their incredible work from beginning to end, and thanks to everyone in the Creative Writing Department at the University of North Carolina, Wilmington. Thanks to my dear friend Tomi Ljungberg, who filled me in on the workings of a Thoroughbred retirement center. And thanks to David and Hadley, who believe in a better world.

the boy i love

One

I could tell you that the trouble between Allie and me started with Tim Greenlaw, but that wouldn't be completely true. If I'm going to be honest (and what's the point of telling this story if I'm not going to be honest?), it's never been easy having a best friend who looks like Allie. Not that I'm the worst-looking girl in the world. I'm fine, I guess, if you don't count my thighs, or the fact that I look way younger than my age. But really that seems like the tiniest little piece of it, because Allie was beautiful a long time before any serious problems cropped up. So I would have to say that the moment everything truly began to change was my run-in with the alligator. When I say alligator, I am not talking about a school mascot, or a stuffed toy, or some kid with a corny nickname. I mean the green and scaly variety, complete with eighty sharp teeth and two beady eyes. A real, live alligator, nearly seven feet long from head to tail.

It happened at the end of my first day at Williamsport High. I'd been waiting for this day all summer, but let me tell you: huge disappointment. After six hours in that big brick building, I felt like I never should have left the Cutty River School. See, originally I'd switched schools so Allie and I could stay together, because *she* was switching schools, but once my parents said I could go, I got pretty amped up about it. So for weeks I'd been playing it through in my head, all the new friends I'd make, the cute new guys I'd meet, and all the fun we'd have. But that first day, the one single person who talked to me at all was Allie. I guess we should have figured that turning up as new sophomores in a school of about eighty million kids, where everyone else had started out as freshmen, would put us at a disadvantage. Stupidly I figured Allie's prettiness would draw people to us. Then I would keep them around with my talkative good humor. That combination had always served us pretty well in the past, but today not so much. For one thing, we barely had any classes together. For another, even when we *were* together, hardly anyone so much as glanced in our direction.

Allie didn't live in Leeville anymore, so I rode the school bus home alone. It let me out at the end of our dirt road, which was a good twenty-minute drive from Williamsport. On the bus it was more like forty minutes with all the stops. I was feeling mighty low and lonesome, and also mighty glad to be back home. My dad's family has lived on this property for generations. It used to be a rice and cotton plantation, surrounded by a bunch of other plantations, but over the years most people have sold off their land and moved. So it wasn't as wild as it used to be. In fact, just two miles away was a new housing development called Cutty River Landing, with a bunch of brick houses, plus a pool and tennis courts.

But you'd never know that suburbia lived so close, because the dirt drive to our farmhouse felt like a piece of the old, forgotten South. And I don't mean before the Civil War. I mean about way back a thousand years ago, when there weren't any roads at all, just native paths down by the river. Above my head the branches of live oaks curled together, Spanish moss dripping from their bark. We had longleaf pines, and trumpet tulip trees, and fruit trees—every once in a while I'd get bombed by an overripe loquat falling to the ground. In the midafternoon heat I could still smell the lingering scent of last night's jasmine. The Cutty River ran beside the road, slow and muddy. I could hear Daisy, our big black German shepherd, barking up near the house. In a few days she would figure out my schedule and sit waiting for the bus at the end of the road. Daisy was good like that. Through the trees on the other side of the river, I could see my mom's horses grazing on the hill. Just the sight of them made me feel better than I had all day.

And then, one of those loquats fell into the river. It hit the water with such a sharp little splash I turned my head to look. That's when I saw it. An alligator. Just . . . floating there. Where, as far as I knew, there had never been an alligator before. And like I said, it was a nearly seven-foot-long alligator. I swear its two black eyes, floating just above the water, were staring right at me.

Dang. I dropped my backpack and ran for the house. "Mom!" I screamed. I'd never been so scared in my whole life. "Mom!" I screamed again.

She came running down from the barn, and my dad came slamming through the screen door onto the front porch. Daisy raced toward me, barking. We all met up at the foot of the porch steps.

"There's an alligator in the river!"

And then, because I was afraid, and overwhelmed, and it was hotter than anything, I decided to be truly dramatic. I put the back of my hand to my forehead and pretended to faint, dropping to the ground like a real southern belle. My parents knelt beside me. I pushed myself up on my elbows and started laughing. For a minute we all sat there, Daisy barking and panting, the three of us laughing our heads off.

"But hey," I finally said. "I wasn't kidding about the alligator."

* * *

Now, it's certainly not unheard-of to find alligators in North Carolina. Some places have plenty of them, but only to the south and east of Williamsport. At least that used to be the case, before I stumbled upon mine. So Dad called up his colleagues from the forest service and the university, and before we knew it a reporter from the *Williamsport Sun-News* and a film crew from the local TV station were in our drive. Don't get too excited about the TV part—it's about the cheesiest news show you can possibly imagine. If I hadn't seen an alligator, the lead story that night would probably have been about a tower of canned peas toppling over at Costco. Still, it was pretty cool, getting out of all my chores so I could stand by the river (well, as close as I dared, given that there was a seven-foot alligator in it) and be interviewed on camera.

"I was just walking down the road like I always do," I said, pointing at the water. The cameraman scrambled down the bank, way closer than I ever would have gotten. The alligator just floated there, looking barely alive, definitely not thinking it was any kind of news. Later that evening, watching me on TV, Dad said that when I pointed at the alligator, I looked like a game show hostess pointing to a prize.

After all the excitement, we had a late dinner. "Wren," my mother said, piling brussels sprouts onto my plate, "I didn't even get to ask you about your first day of school."

I shrugged and said, "It was okay," trying not to let too much disappointment creep into my voice. But I could tell from their faces they'd already figured out it was not what I'd been hoping for, so I added, "At least Allie and I have American history together. And lunch. It would be torture to sit alone eating lunch in that huge cafeteria."

"First days are always hard," Dad said. "It'll get better. You'll see."

I bit my lip. Dad was the kind of person who would be perfectly happy sitting alone at a lunch table as long as he could identify whatever bird was trilling outside the window.

"You just have to give it some time," my mom chimed in. "By this time next week, everyone will know how truly and completely wonderful you are."

It was nice of them to comfort me, especially since they never wanted me to go to Williamsport in the first place. Cutty River was the charter school here in Leeville, and it was smaller and more progressive, so plenty of people from Williamsport were willing to make the commute. But Cutty River didn't have all the great sports and arts programs that Williamsport did. And I really wanted to try out for plays. The plays at Williamsport were a huge deal; people from all over the area would come to see them. My parents had been taking me since I was itty-bitty. They said if I was interested in theater I could take acting lessons after school, but I had begged and pleaded and finally won them over. So I appreciated them not saying right away that I could always go back to Cutty River if I wanted. I smiled at my mom and took a bite of brussels sprouts. Everyone always says they hate brussels sprouts, but she roasts them with maple syrup and fish sauce, which may sound weird to you, but it's actually quite delicious.

After dinner I called Allie and told her to stay up and watch the news. I didn't tell her why. "Just watch the whole thing," I said. "Get your parents to watch it too."

Allie said she would, but instead of asking me why, she said, "But Wren, guess who I saw at Kilwin's after school?" And before I could answer, she said, "Tim Greenlaw."

"Tim Greenlaw!" Tim had been a year ahead of us at Cutty River until he left to go to Williamsport in ninth grade. Even in middle school he was super athletic, and super blond, and Allie and I'd both had huge crushes on him. He never spoke to either of us, not one single time.

"He's even cuter than he used to be," Allie promised. "Much taller. And I think he smiled at me. I hope we see him at school tomorrow."

"Me too," I said. Truthfully, I had grown out of my crush on Tim. The boy I loved was my guitar teacher, even if he was in college. And anyway, even in middle school Allie had liked Tim more than I did. So I said, "You'll have to go out with Tim. I can't cheat on Ry."

Allie laughed. We had a running discussion on how to make Ry forget our age difference and fall in love with me. Then Allie said, "But Tim's so gorgeous. He'd never like me."

I rolled my eyes at this. Allie's always done that, pretended she didn't know how pretty she was. In that moment I felt like she just wanted me to compliment her, and for some reason I didn't feel like it. Sometimes I am a bad friend that way.

Even though she couldn't see me, Allie had a way of sensing she'd lost my attention. "Come on," she said. "Tell me why I have to watch the news." I broke down and told her about the alligator. She whistled. "Your parents are never going to let you walk down that driveway again."

"Sure they will," I said, even though she was probably right. My parents are just a tad bit overprotective. They always have been. A few years ago they let Allie and me camp out at the Civil War fort down on Old Farthing Road. They promised we could go all by ourselves, but when I crawled out of the tent in the morning, there was my dad, sitting in a lawn chair, a crumpled bag of Krispy Kreme doughnuts at his feet and a rifle across his lap.

"Daddy," I said, hugely annoyed, my hands on my hips. "What do you think you're doing?"

He blinked at me a couple of times, then said, "Protecting what's precious, darlin'. I'm protecting what's precious."

At the time it'd made me mad that he'd gone back on his word. But now, sitting on my bed talking to Allie, the memory made me smile. She was right, of course. There was no way I'd be walking down that road alone tomorrow.

The next morning, sure enough, Dad and I took his Jeep down to meet the bus. He let me drive. I kind of hoped he'd let me drive all the way to school. Even though I'd turned sixteen last week, I still only had a learner's permit, so I needed a licensed driver in the car with me. But when I suggested this to Dad, he said, "You made a deal, Wren."

I tried not to snort at this. The deal: I'd promised that if they let me switch schools, I would take the bus every day. Dad thought it would be good for me to have to get to the end of the road on time, because in his opinion I had problems with punctuality. He also said that even after I got my license, it would be a good while before they would be comfortable with me driving into Williamsport on my own. Overprotective, like I said. Still, even if I did have my license, we didn't exactly have money lying around for an extra car, so there hardly seemed a point in hurrying down to the DMV.

While we waited for the bus, Dad told me that the biologists and forest service people needed to decide whether they should move the alligator or let the species expand its territory. No matter what they decided, I wasn't sure if I would ever walk down the road by myself again. And thanks to Mr. Alligator, I knew my days of swimming in the Cutty River were over for good, even if the mercury rose to two hundred degrees.

But guess what? When I got on the bus, it turned out I'd become a celebrity! It seemed everyone on the bus had heard about our alligator. Who knew so many kids watched the news? Even the people who hadn't seen me on TV knew about it. Practically everyone leaned out the open windows, trying to look down the river and spot the gator. When I sat down and the bus pulled away, about ten kids—most of them juniors and seniors—crowded around, asking me questions. I told them about how that loquat fell off the tree and then I saw the alligator floating in the water. I held my hands out wide to show them how big it was, wiggling my fingers to show it was even longer than my arms would go.

"God," one girl said. "I would've run so fast!"

"That's what I did," I told her. "My dad said I looked like the Bionic Woman coming up the driveway." I didn't mention that I'd screamed for my mom the whole way.

During this conversation, I noticed one guy hanging over the seat a couple of rows closer to the driver, watching me. It kinda seemed like he was more interested in me than what I said about the alligator. Not knowing I would be getting so much attention today, I hadn't put much effort into what I was wearing. I had on a sleeveless Fresh Produce sundress that essentially looked like an oversize T-shirt, and my hair was in a sloppy ponytail. It took a full minute for me to realize that it was Tim Greenlaw looking at me. Not only that, but Allie had been right: He was much taller and even cuter than he'd been at the Cutty River School. Tim Greenlaw looked like he'd spent the whole summer surfing at Wilbur Beach, with this super-blond hair that flopped across his forehead, and the perfect number of freckles. And he had a very smiley way about him, even when he wasn't smiling. That might not make any sense, but I think it had something to do with his eyes. For some reason he always just looked like a happy person, thinking secret happy thoughts.

Tim saw me staring back at him and waved. "Hey, Wren," he said.

Because I am an idiot who never thinks before she speaks, I blurted out, "You remember me?"

He smiled, a slow and self-aware smile like he was used to turning girls into morons. "Well, sure," he said. "I didn't get amnesia after Cutty River." I think he felt bad for me when my face turned red, because he added, "Also, I saw you on the news last night."

It was nice of him to try, but that didn't help. My cheeks burned all the way into Williamsport.

* * *

I got over my embarrassment pretty quick, though, because the rest of the morning went pretty much like the bus ride. Even the teachers stopped me in the hall to ask about the alligator. The story was also in the *Williamsport Sun-News*. By the time I met Allie for lunch at a picnic table outside, I was exhausted from all the attention.

"Well, hello to you, Miss Famous," Allie said, scooching close. "Everybody's been talking about that alligator, and seeing you on TV. I told one girl you were my best friend, and I don't think she even believed me. She thought I was just trying to curry favor." This last is the kind of expression Allie uses all the time, probably because her parents are professors.

Allie looked much more done up than usual. Yesterday had been just as much a letdown for her as it was for me. But unlike me, this hadn't kept her from making an effort. She wore this flouncy little skirt that made her legs look four miles long, a tank top, and a cool string of clear and purple beads, plus she'd straightened her hair. It wasn't like her to try so hard, and I could tell she was determined to get noticed. Allie was used to people paying lots of attention to her on account of her looks. For example, last July when she went to visit her grandmother in New York City, a modeling scout spotted her sifting through the Ralph Lauren sales rack at Bloomingdale's. The scout wanted her to make an appointment for test shots, but Allie's parents said no, which was probably the biggest disappointment in Allie's entire life. Allie still carried that woman's business card with her everywhere she went, and I noticed her tapping her fingers on the side of her little purse, probably to remind herself it was there.

But for the first time since we'd been friends, it wasn't Allie's looks that finally got us attention. It was my alligator. I barely had a chance to tell her she looked great when two guys helped themselves to the bench on the other side of our table. One of them was from our American history class; his name was Devon Kelly. The other one was . . . Tim Greenlaw. Allie pinched my hand under the table.

"Hey," Devon said. "It's Alligator Girl."

You wouldn't think it, but between the two of us, Allie is the shy one. She waited for me to say something back to Devon. But seriously, how much more could I possibly say about an alligator? Mostly they just lie around in the water, not even bothering to swish their tails.

This kid Devon sounded like a Yankee, but I am half Yankee on my mother's side, so this did not bother me at all. Plus, he had this casual, friendly way about him, like everything was just a little bit of a joke. I could tell Allie was pretty thrilled that they'd come over, and I didn't want to blow this chance for her. Or myself, for that matter. Unfortunately, I couldn't think of anything cleverer to say than, "I'm Wren, and this is my friend Allie."

Allie smiled at Tim. She is very exotic-looking, with glossy dark hair and gigantic gray eyes shaped like Cleopatra's. Devon stared straight at her when he said, "Well, hello there, Allie and Wren."

I noted how he gave Allie top billing, which was pretty much par for the course. Devon asked me a couple of questions about the TV crew, then told us he was having a party on Saturday night. "It's on the beach by my house," he said. The invitation was for both of us, but he was still staring at Allie. This didn't bother me as I loved Ry, my guitar teacher. Meanwhile, Allie ignored Devon's staring. She kept zeroing right in on Tim, who kind of smiled back at her in a polite way.

"So you'll come?" Devon said.

"Sure," Allie finally piped up. "You bet. We'll come, for sure."

Devon and Tim got up and sauntered toward the gym, while Allie and I cleared our food away. "Well, well," she said, as we tossed out the garbage from our lunch—which in both cases included most of the lunch itself. "It looks like there are all kinds of benefits to having an alligator in your backyard." She had the happiest little smile on her face, and even though it was nearly a hundred degrees out, I could tell in her head she was already wearing Tim's football jacket.

As we walked back toward school, Allie had a little

bounce in her step. We were definitely having a better second day than first. Even though I wasn't at all sure that my parents would let me go to Devon's, I wasn't going to spoil Allie's excitement by telling her.

Two

Allie and I have been best friends since kindergarten.
She used to live out in the boondocks like us, but last year
her parents finally got sick of the commute to the university,
so they moved to Williamsport. Allie never had to tell them
about wanting to be a cheerleader in order to switch schools,
not like me with the acting. When we were kids, Allie won
tons of gymnastics awards, but she got so tall she couldn't
do it competitively anymore. Cheerleading seemed like a
good new sport for her, but being intellectuals and feminists,
her parents did not exactly approve. Not that they would
put their foot down about it. They just weren't particularly
encouraging.

As for my family, we are stuck in Leeville for good. Back
when they were first married, my mom turned Dad's old
family plantation into the North Carolina Thoroughbred
Retirement Center. The original pillared grand house had

burned down during the Civil War, so we live in the regular old farmhouse that was built to replace it. All the other buildings except the stables were torn down years ago. My mom rescues horses that would otherwise be headed to the glue factory, rehabilitates them, and finds them new homes. That last part is theoretical, because Mom is so picky about where they go. Usually the horses stay with us for a long time, if not forever, and we generally have about fifteen of them. This whole setup might sound like a whole lot of fun to you, and I guess it was before the economy collapsed. But taking care of horses is pretty expensive, what with feed and vet bills, so even before that, my parents always sweated bullets over their bills. Mom could never bear to turn one single horse away, even though the farm was refinanced to the hilt.

However, living on a horse farm does have plenty of items in the plus column, especially my favorite horse, Pandora. Whenever anyone asks what I would take with me to a desert island (and people ask this more often than you might think), I always say Pandora. She is beautiful and gentle and fast, and has been here with us since longer back than I can remember. There is no amount of horse manure I wouldn't shovel, or tack I wouldn't polish, as long as I could ride Pandora every day of my life.

After my second day at Williamsport High, my mom was waiting for me in her station wagon when I got off the bus. Aunt Holly hopped out of the passenger seat to give me a hug.

"I didn't know you were coming," I told her.

"Well, who else was going to protect you from that gator?" Holly said, and I laughed. She laughed too, but there was a wistful note to it. Holly was my dad's younger sister, and for the last few months she always looked sad, like she might cry any minute, ever since she called off her wedding.

Holly got back into the car, and I climbed into the rear seat with Daisy, who had to sniff and lick at me to make sure no damage had been done while I'd been gone. Our family nickname for Daisy is Hellhound. She weighs almost a hundred pounds, is pitch black, and has the deepest, most ferocious bark in the world. Mom saved Daisy from doggy death row. She landed there because she bit a FedEx delivery man. You'd think a mother might have been cautious about adopting a dog that had a history of biting, but no. The truth is my mother is the kind of person who should have had ten kids, but instead she had me and three miscarriages. She says that after the last miscarriage, she realized Dad and I were all she really needed in this world, and I almost never point out that she also seems to need a lot of expensive animals whose owners want to toss them away.

Mom started the car and turned back up our driveway. Last night Dad kept saying that alligators were usually not aggressive toward humans. Mom and I had not taken a whole lot of comfort in the word "usually." After all, alligators *usually* didn't travel northwest of Williamsport. Clearly this reptile was what my dad would call an outlier, and I would not be walking up or down our driveway anytime soon. But at that moment the main thing on my mind was how to get my parents to let me go to that party on Saturday night.

"Mom," I said, leaning forward from the backseat. "Do you remember a boy named Tim Greenlaw from the Cutty River School?"

"It doesn't ring a bell," she said, and of course it wouldn't. We had never done anything social with him, and I generally did not discuss my crushes with my parents.

"He was a grade ahead of us," I told her. "Allie and I had lunch with him today, he's at Williamsport now too."

"That's nice," Mom said.

"Anyway," I hurried on, like if I spoke fast enough she would say yes without thinking, "he has a friend who lives at Wilbur Beach who's having a party Saturday night, and Allie and me are invited. Isn't that great?"

Holly nodded, like she agreed it was great. She looks like my dad and me in that she has brown hair and brown eyes. But lately my dad had started wearing glasses, and Holly can still see just fine. Plus, her face is completely covered with square, pale freckles, which personally I find very wonderful. I'm a big freckle fan, and I have always found it disappointing not to have any myself. Holly is a hospital chaplain at a medical center in Raleigh, so her whole job is comforting sick people.

"Now wait a minute," Mom said. "Who exactly is throwing this party? Do we know his parents? Will parents even be there?"

"And so it begins," Holly said, laughing a little. "We always knew this day was coming, Elizabeth."

Mom sighed and stopped the car. We got out and started walking to the house. "I don't know, Wren," Mom said. "In Wilbur Beach? Your dad's not going to like it."

My heart began to sink. Wilbur Beach is the richest town around here, and these days my parents have a grudge against anyone who doesn't spend every waking moment worrying about money. Whenever my mom sees a Mercedes or BMW on the road, her face gets very dark.

But Holly, oh thank you, Holly. She said, "Come on, Elizabeth, let her go. What's the harm? Let her go."

Mom didn't argue. I knew she wouldn't. Everybody had been treating Holly with kid gloves since the end of her engagement. See, James Galveston was a doctor in the burn unit at her hospital in Raleigh, but he grew up here in Leeville. He was supersmart and super nice. As far as I'm concerned, he and Holly have been together forever; they've known each other since high school. Back then the Cutty River School didn't even exist, so come to think of it, they'd probably started dating at Williamsport High when Holly was a freshman and James was a junior. Their whole lives, everybody always knew that they would end up together. They were just one of those perfect couples: both of them sweet, nice people who wanted to devote their lives to helping others. But last year James's father died, which inspired his sister to start researching their family, and she had found out that their ancestors had been slaves. Being that they were African American, this was not a big shock. But then . . . it turned out that their great-great-great-grandmother had . . . I can hardly stand to say it. But she belonged to our family. *Belonged to our family*. It sounds so weird and awful. It *is* so weird and awful. Just thinking it gives me this sharp and terrible pain in my stomach, and I have to push it out of my head very quickly.

Holly and James tried to move past this discovery—I mean, it was hardly Holly's fault—but they just couldn't. For one thing, the wedding had been planned at our farm (we had never been happy calling it a plantation, and obviously, now this was even more the case). James just got more and more weirded out, and then the question came up as to the possibility of what if they were somehow *related*, and everybody just became more guilty and more confused, and finally they called the whole thing quits. It was the saddest thing in the world and also—in my opinion—the most unfair. It wasn't Holly's fault her ancestors owned slaves.

She was the nicest, kindest person I'd ever known in my whole life. All she ever did was help out people of every stripe and color and situation. If she'd been around during slave days, you can bet she would have been working full-time for the Underground Railroad, escorting everyone north. She was the last person who should have to pay for someone else's crimes.

Thinking about this, I felt a wave of sadness. I was getting my party, but Holly didn't get hers. I headed upstairs to change into my barn clothes, then grabbed a couple of carrots from the refrigerator. And even though I knew my mother had an afternoon of forking straw planned for me, and even though I felt plenty bad for Holly and James, I couldn't help but walk with a little bounce in my step. Because I knew that all my mother and father wanted to do these days was cheer Holly up. If it cheered her up to know I was headed to a party at the beach, then you can bet on Saturday night that's exactly where I'd be going.

On Friday afternoon I couldn't wait to see Ry, my guitar teacher. He had been at Tanglewood in Massachusetts all summer, teaching at a music camp. I came downstairs carrying my guitar case, wearing a cutoff denim skirt and a tank top, my hair loose. When I got to the foot of the stairs, Dad told me to march right back up and put on something decent.

"And don't even think about wearing something like that

to your party tomorrow," he ordered. I swallowed my anger
but closed the door to my room gently. I wanted to slam it,
hard, but knew that anything seeming rebellious could end
up in exactly what he wanted, which was an excuse to go
back on his promise to let me go to the party on Saturday.
I came back down in baggy khaki shorts, a white sleeveless
oxford, and my hair in a ponytail.

"Happy now?" I said, trying not to sound sarcastic.

"Ecstatic," Dad said. He opened the front door for me.
"You look prettier like that anyway," he said, and I rolled my
eyes. This was the man who had chosen my mother, after all,
who owned no shoes except flip-flops, sneakers, and riding
boots. Dad's favorite outfits for males and females alike con-
sisted of flannel shirts and beat-up Levi's.

Maybe to make up for annoying me, Dad let me drive to
the music store. He hated driving on real streets with me
more than anything in the world, so there was a lot of yelling my name and covering his eyes, plus he had this imagi-
nary brake of his own that he kept stomping on.

At the music store I hauled my guitar out of the backseat,
and Dad looked mighty relieved as he jumped over into the
driver's seat. I waited for him to pull away before I took my
hair down and tied my shirt so that just a tiny bit of midriff
showed.

"Hey there, Wren," Ry said. I smiled at him. It's true I'd
had a little crush on Tim Greenlaw when I was just a child.

But Ry made me feel like a girl from a romance novel. Allie didn't think he was handsome at all, but that didn't bother me. He could play all kinds of instruments, including the piano, a twelve-string guitar, and a Dobro. Plus he could sing, plus he recited poetry in this voice that was calm and excited at the exact same time. He would do it to make a point, like a poem could actually clarify something, a thought or an idea. I know this must sound completely corny, but when Ry does it, it's not corny at all. It's just totally cool.

Ry closed the door to the lesson room behind us, which may sound promising, but unfortunately, one wall was a huge soundproof window so everyone in the store could look in and see us having our lesson. Ry and I took out our guitars and started tuning. At least he did. I always just pretended to be tuning my guitar until he finally took it away from me and did it himself. "Have you been working on 'John Barleycorn'?" Ry asked, tightening up my C string.

"Yes," I lied. I almost never practiced between lessons. Ry pretended not to know this, but then he would make some comment that should sound like a compliment—about my natural ability—that clearly implied I didn't put in any effort whatsoever.

He handed me back my guitar. "Aren't you going to ask me about my first week of tenth grade?" I said.

"Are you in tenth grade already?" Ry said. "I forgot you'd got so old."

"Shut up," I said. I hated to be reminded of how young I looked, especially by Ry. We played the song through once, with him shouting out the chord progressions, and me making all kinds of mistakes. I hoped he would come sit by me and show me the chords by putting his hands over my fingers, the way he used to, but he just kept to his own bench on the opposite side of the small space. After a little while we quit and worked on easier songs, but at the end of the lesson we went back to "John Barleycorn." After the first verse I gave up trying to play and just sang with Ry, keeping up the melody while he came in with all kinds of cool harmonies.

"Dang," Ry said, when we finished singing. "You sure do have a pretty voice, Wren."

And that compliment was enough to keep me smiling all the rest of the day.

Here was the deal we made so Allie and I could go to the party. It took about five phone conversations between our parents to work it out. My parents and Aunt Holly and I would drive into Williamsport and pick up Allie. Then the three of them would drop us off, and while we were at the party, they'd eat dinner at this beach restaurant my mother loved but never got to go to.

"A long dinner," I said. "A really, really long dinner."

"A pretty long dinner," my mom said.

"Long enough," my dad added.

After dinner they'd go listen to music at the tiki bar and then come get us. They would call when they got to the beach entry. I made them swear up and down that they would not set foot anywhere near the actual party.

"And I'm borrowing a Breathalyzer from Ken Pories," Dad said on Saturday morning. Ken Pories was one of the police officers who worked with the forest service. "You and Allie are both going to blow into it the minute you get in my car."

"You are not serious," I groaned. We were standing in front of our house. I had just gotten back from a horseback ride in the horrible heat with Mom. Sweat and dirt rolled down my face, and the back of my neck itched.

"You'll find out after the party, won't you?" he asked.

Grrrr.

Allie and I had been checking in all day long about what we were going to wear and how we were going to act. Allie was ecstatic—she'd found out that Tim Greenlaw used to go out with a girl named Caroline Jones, but they had broken up, so he was officially available. But I was just psyched about being invited to a cool party so soon. It made me feel like my life was finally happening *now* instead of just in day-dreams, and that everything for the next three years might just work out okay. So I spent an unusual amount of time in front of the mirror, straightening my hair. Unfortunately, I have never been any good at doing hair, so I ended up giving up and pulling it into a high ponytail. I didn't put on any makeup, partly because Dad wouldn't allow it and partly because after my ride with Mom, my cheeks were nicely pink. I put on my Anthropologie dress and knew I would feel good about myself till I saw Allie walk out the door looking like a supermodel. Here's what I've found works best in such moments of jealousy: Just stop and admit that's what you feel. Don't fight it or try to give it a different name. It may be ugly, but if you don't resist it or make excuses for it, it passes pretty quick.

My main worry when I came down the stairs was that Dad would send me back up to change. Through the screen door I could see my parents and Holly standing together at the bottom of the porch steps. They all sounded just sad, Holly's voice full of tears. Her back was to me, but I could see her wave her hand in a sweeping gesture toward our land.

"Maybe it's just as well," Holly was saying. "It was all built on blood anyway, blood and shame. Maybe we should just let it go."

"But the horses." I could hear my mom's voice catch, not wanting to argue with Holly, but not able to stop protecting what mattered most to her—her horses, her strays. Speaking of which, a one-eyed tabby who'd have nothing to do with anyone but Mom wound its creaky body around her ankles as she spoke. "Where would all the horses go?" my mom said, and my dad put his arm around her shoulders.

What were they talking about? Giving up our *farm*? I froze at the thought, and at not wanting them to know I was listening.

I heard Holly say, "I love what you do here, Elizabeth, I truly do. But wouldn't it be better, more fitting, if we just gave the place back to the people who worked it? We could track down all the ancestors of all the slaves and just deed it over."

"You can't give away what you don't own anymore," Dad said. His voice sounded dark, and I thought that was a very odd thing to say. Whose else would this place be if not ours? I hated the way Dad's shoulders slumped, and the way Mom's neck tensed, and I couldn't stand hearing another word. I pushed the door open with as much noise as I could make, knowing my presence would stop the conversation cold.

The three of them turned. Holly whistled. "Look at you, pretty girl."

Dad shot her an evil look, and I held my breath. But he didn't say anything about my outfit, so we all piled into Holly's car—which was generally free of dog hair and farm implements and therefore a much more pleasant ride—and headed to the party.

I was so glad that Holly came with us. If it hadn't been for her, my dad would have insisted on walking over to the dunes and checking out the party himself. I realized this when we pulled up to the beach access and he took off his seat belt at the same time Allie and I did.

"What are you doing?" I asked. "You don't need to get out of the car."

"That's your opinion," Dad said. Allie and I looked at each other, panicked. If Dad was going to escort us to the party like we were a pair of three-year-olds, there was no point in even going. We would be laughed out of the party, the school, maybe even the entire state.

"Oh, come on, Joe," Holly said. "Do you have no memory at all? Let the girls go to their party without you embarrassing them to death. We're just going to be gone a couple hours. What could happen?"

"It's funny you of all people would say that," Dad said, "with the stories you tell from the hospital."

The next rescue came from a surprising source, my mom. She said, "We can't follow Wren around forever, Joe."

"I don't see why not," Dad grumbled. But he stayed put while Allie and I scrambled out of the car. Just as I had expected, Allie looked amazing, even though all she wore was cutoffs and an Izod T-shirt. Have I mentioned that she's about a foot taller than I am, even though she's almost a year younger?

"We'll call when we leave the tiki bar," Mom said through the open window. "You'd better be right here waiting for us, or I won't be able to keep him from crashing your party."

We stood there and waved as Holly's car pulled away. Then we turned to each other for last-minute check-overs. Allie gave me some lip gloss and adjusted my ponytail. Her hair looked perfect, with this shiny little barrette in it. She had the much better idea going casual. I felt like a jerk wearing a dress to a beach party.

"Does this dress make me look like I'm trying too hard?" I asked.

"That dress," she said, "makes you look gorgeous. So quit worrying."

I reached out and squeezed her hand, grateful. From the other side of the dunes, we could already see smoke from the bonfire rising in the air. I saw a flock of skimmers, flying just below its white strands. We could hear the ocean and smell the seaweed. Our first high school party! Allie slipped off her flip-flops and stashed them under a yucca plant, but I kept my sandals on. They had a little wedge heel, which I figured I could manage even on the sand, and I needed all the help I could get.

By now the sun had started its dip toward the ocean, and I was glad that Allie and I could make our appearance in dusky sort-of light. We headed over to the fire, where a good number of people were already gathered. The first people we saw were a bunch of girls, juniors and seniors, I guessed. A couple of them wore bikini tops with skirts or shorts, and I had another flash of regretting my dress.

The girls looked us up and down, then smiled at one another and turned back to their conversation like we didn't exist. For all they knew we had just wandered in off the street. Allie and I circled around the fire, looking for anyone we knew. A lot of the kids held red plastic cups that no doubt were filled with beer. There seemed to be a pretty steady line of people traveling between the fire and the dunes. I figured they had a keg stashed back there. Allie and I looked at each other, then shrugged. I hadn't seen anything in the car that looked like it could be Ken Pories's Breathalyzer. Still, I wasn't going to take a chance and get grounded for the rest of my life.

"I'd rather be in control of myself," Allie said, and I nodded, even though it seemed like the other people at the party were having plenty of fun being not so much in control. Just then we heard a low whistle as Devon and Tim walked toward us carrying their red plastic cups.

"Hey, hey," Devon said, with his Yankee accent. He sounded so happy to see us, my heart gave an extra little *thump, thump* of excitement. "Look who showed up!"

It may have been getting dark, but I knew Allie well enough to know she was blushing. I had a feeling she felt exactly like I did—excited to be here, but also nervous. Of course the first thing Devon and Tim did was offer us some beer.

"We can't," Allie said. She gathered up her courage and told them about the Breathalyzer.

"That's rough," Devon said. Tim nodded in agreement. So far, one thing I had noticed about Tim, he wasn't much of a talker. Maybe he was shy, like Allie. "Look," Devon said, pointing toward the skimmers who waddled on the shore. "The puffins are back."

I kept myself from laughing at this. The skimmers, with their crazy orange bills, did look weirdly Arctic. But I had never heard anyone mistake them for puffins before. Allie had spent enough time with my dad to know exactly what those birds were called, and I waited, giving her a chance to impress Tim with what she knew. But she didn't say anything, so after a moment I said, "Those aren't puffins. They're skimmers."

"Yeah?" Devon said.

He sounded slightly less friendly, like I'd annoyed him. I know I can be a little obnoxious that way, so I made my voice apologetic when I said, "My dad's a songbird expert for the forest service," trying to make it sound more like an excuse for my bad behavior than information.

"Are those songbirds?" Devon said, all nice again.

"They're a kind of gull." I didn't tell him the real order name, which is Charadriiformes. I may not be shy like Allie, but I'm not a total social idiot. Only a partial one.

"A songbird expert," Tim said. "What a cool job."

I shrugged like I didn't agree, but inside I smiled. Allie shifted next to me, and I felt bad that they weren't paying more attention to her. Even though Allie wasn't talking, she kept staring at Tim in this way that almost looked like pleading. *Like me*, Allie's eyes kept saying to Tim. *Notice me*.

We all stood there, suddenly out of things to say. I wondered if there was anything to drink besides beer. Not because I was especially thirsty. It would just be better to have something to do with my hands. So I asked.

"Sure," Devon said. He and Tim jogged off toward the keg, with Allie and me following a few steps behind. I tried not to trip in my sandals. It was getting dark, so there were only a few nonparty people on the beach—some of them walking hand in hand, and some of them letting their kids have one last beach romp before bedtime. I could just make out the outline of one couple, pressed together and whispering. Don't ask me why, but out of nowhere I suddenly imagined that being me and Tim. With Allie standing next to me, liking him so much, I felt an instant surge of guilt. Still, I imagined it. Or maybe just imagined imagining it, as, to be honest, it seemed almost impossible. Maybe that sounds immature for sixteen. But my parents had hardly ever let me out of their sight. I'd never been allowed to date—not that I really had a chance to challenge that rule, since no one had ever asked me out. Other than a few scattered games of spin the bottle, I had never even kissed a guy, and spin-the-bottle kisses don't count.

Devon opened up a cooler full of soda and bottled water.

Allie and I both asked for water. She kept on staring at Tim, her hair blowing around in the breeze and her face all shy and vulnerable. How could he not fall in love with her right on the spot?

"So," Allie said. She sipped her water, and I knew it took every bit of confidence for her to start a conversation. "Are y'all going out for football?"

"Allie's going to be a cheerleader," I said.

"Going to try to be one," she corrected.

"I'm already on varsity," Devon said. He clapped Tim on the back. "So was this loser until he decided he wanted to try out for the school play."

"Hey, I'm trying out too," I said, way too fast and way too excited. "I'm so bummed it's a musical. I can hardly sing at all." This last was a lie, and as soon as it was out of my mouth, I wondered why I'd said it.

"She can too sing," Allie said. "Wait till you hear her."

By this point the sun had set. The water had gone dark but had a pretty shimmer on top of it from the moon, and lights from passing boats.

Devon said, "Yeah, it's always the girls who say they can't sing who have the great voices. But this guy." He gave Tim a playful little shove. "I don't know why Tim wants to wreck a perfectly good winning streak so he can sing songs with a bunch of faggots."

Allie and I both did double takes. At Cutty River, you

could get suspended for a whole week just for using a word like "faggot." The teachers would've called it hate speech. I looked over at Tim like I expected him to melt right there on the ground. But he didn't, just took a sip of his beer as if Devon hadn't said anything at all.

I almost said something to Devon. I swear I did. But Allie was widening her eyes at me in a way that said *please, please, do NOT say anything.* So I kept my mouth shut. It was Devon's party, after all, and he'd been nice enough to invite us. And if Tim didn't care, why should I?

I looked over at all the kids crowded around the fire. It seemed like fifty more people had arrived just since we came to get our drinks. Some had brought guitars, so we headed back there, sidling our way through the crowd to stand right in front of the flames. There was a girl sitting with the guitar players, and she started singing along with them. I thought she was pretty good. I wondered if I would ever be that brave, to sing in front of all these people. I stood there for a second, imagining how it would feel to not only be at this party but be the absolute center of attention.

As this thought formed in my head, I had no way of knowing that in another moment I *would* be the absolute center of attention, but for a much less positive reason than singing a song. Because just then a group of three drunk girls pushed through the crowd to get close to the fire. One of them (I found out later it was Tim's old girlfriend, Caroline Jones) tripped and reached out to grab me for balance. Maybe if I'd been wearing sneakers, or bare feet, I would have been less wobbly. Or maybe since I never saw her coming I wouldn't have stood a chance anyway. But what did happen was, I pitched directly forward. My water bottle flew out of my right hand. I saw the flames coming at my face. Later everyone said it happened in the blink of an eye, but to me it felt like slow motion. I reached out my left hand to catch myself. Unfortunately, the only place to put it at that point was straight onto the burning logs of the fire.

"Wren!" Allie screamed. "Oh my God, Wren!"

I thought at first it was her who grabbed the back of my dress and pulled me out of the fire. But it was Tim. One second later and probably my hair and head would have gone up in flames. In that moment, however, I could not appreciate my good fortune, because my hand hurt worse than I ever knew anything could possibly hurt in this world, and the only thing I heard was my own voice, screaming.

Three

Screaming, screaming, screaming, plus blinding pain.
Plus other voices screaming, particularly Allie's. Someone
told her to call an ambulance, and because I hadn't quite
humiliated myself enough, I started yelling, "No! It's too
much money! We can't afford it! We can't afford it!" For all
my new classmates to hear.

The whole party had turned into total chaos. Allie had to
fill me in later on some of what happened, like Devon and a
bunch of his friends rushing off to hide the keg in the dune
grass, and Caroline—the girl who knocked me into the fire—
puking into the ocean and crying her eyes out from the guilt.
Allie said she kept saying, "I'm so sorry," and "Is she okay?"
in between retches. I was not aware of any of this, because I
was locked in a world of total pain. Tim grabbed my hand
and held it up above my head (he told me after that he knew
from Boy Scouts that it needed to stay above my heart).

"You should let us call an ambulance," he said.

And I yelled back, "No, No, No."

Tim could see it was no use, so he ripped off his T-shirt, doused it with bottled water, and wrapped it loosely around my hand. Somebody tried to get me to take a swig from a bottle of whiskey. My hand hurt so bad I would have tried anything, but at the first taste I just gagged and spit it out all over the sand. Everyone was shouting at us to stick my hand into the ocean, or put it on ice, but Tim kept shaking his head.

"Come on," he said. "I've got my mom's car. I'll take you to the hospital."

We were halfway to Williamsport before I realized we'd left Allie back at the beach.

"Don't worry," Tim said. "Someone will give her a ride home. Let's just concentrate on getting you help."

I couldn't concentrate on anything; my hand hurt so bad I almost wanted to die. He told me to keep holding my hand up over my head, and I finally quit worrying about Allie, and the money for an ambulance, and muttered about how I'd ruined the party.

"It's not your fault," Tim kept saying.

"You're so nice," I told him. He reached over and touched my knee. His face looked pale. Even his freckles had disappeared.

When we got to the hospital, they rushed me right past

triage and into a room, where they gave me a shot for the pain. *Thank you* was all I could say to that, and then everything became a blur. At some point I saw Holly's face hovering over me. I forgot that she'd already been in town, and so I decided I must be dying. My hand got wrapped up in a big, moist, gauzy balloon, and I thought how I wouldn't be able to play guitar and maybe I couldn't even try out for the play.

It seems to me that Tim was there for a quite a while—I have a memory of him wearing one of those blue scrub shirts, one of the nurses must have given it to him—but then he disappeared. I found out later that Allie was never there, but for some reason I thought she was, and in my fog I hoped she would get a ride home with Tim, because I knew how happy that would make her.

At some point my parents took me home, but I don't remember that. I just woke up the next morning in my own bed, with my poor hand throbbing away. You would think that burning your hand meant just that—a hurt hand. But I felt worse than if I had the flu. I was nauseous and my head pounded and I couldn't even see clearly. It was like I'd hurt my whole body instead of just my hand.

I yelled for my mom but she didn't answer, and I couldn't hear her moving around the house. Then I realized I couldn't hear her because the air-conditioning was on. My parents tried not to use the air-conditioning much; the fact that they'd turned it on made me realize even more

how bad I must be hurt. I got up and headed for the stairs, cradling my bandaged hand in the crook of my right elbow like it was a little baby. I felt just awful, and my plan was to holler for my mom again when I got to the landing. But before I had a chance to open my mouth, I saw a sight that almost made me forget the pain in my hand, at least for a second: Holly and James, standing inside by the front door. They were talking, but so quietly that I couldn't hear even the sounds of their voices. James had his hand on her shoulder, and Holly was nodding. My heart swelled up—I never knew I could feel so much hope for someone else.

I'm sure I didn't make a noise, but somehow they both sensed I was there as they turned their heads at the same time. James looked solemn. It must have been intense for him, being at our farm again. He'd decided very firmly never to set foot back here. And now he was here, going back on that decision, because—I was sure—of me.

Despite everything he must have been feeling, James smiled. "Wren," he said. "I hear you had an accident."

"Yes, sir, I did," I said. Suddenly standing up became too much for me, and I sank down onto the top step. James removed his hand from Holly's shoulder and took the steps two at a time. When he got to me he sat down too. I automatically put my hand on his knee, and he unwound the bandage carefully.

Have I mentioned that James is the nicest person in the

world, his only possible competition being Holly? He looked at my palm, which was this terrible screaming pink color, with little yellow blisters all over it. My fingertips were pink too. I thought I would throw up just looking at that burn.

"Holly asked me to come over and change the bandage for you," James said. He had this deep voice, like a radio announcer's.

"That was nice of you to come all the way here," I said. And I meant it; it was more than a two-hour drive from Raleigh. He held my hand gingerly, looking at it like it could tell him something.

"It hurts a lot, doesn't it, Wren?"

I nodded. He said I'd have to take pain medication for a few days, and that it hurting so bad was actually a good sign. If it had been a third- or fourth-degree burn, I wouldn't have felt anything at all. He said it didn't even look like a deep second-degree burn, which meant that only the top two layers of skin got hurt—probably because Tim had pulled me out of the fire so quick. But because the burn covered my whole palm and the tips of my fingers, it was major rather than minor, so we had to take it seriously, keeping it clean and cool and watching out for infection.

"Can you . . . stay?" I asked James. "Just to keep an eye on it?"

I heard Holly's footsteps downstairs, walking away. I hoped I hadn't embarrassed her, and I also hoped that she was going to get the pain medicine James had mentioned. I could barely sit still, my hand hurt so bad.

"I'll stick around at least for today," James said. Holly came up the stairs carrying a glass of water, and then handed me two blue pills. I saw her smile at James, a real small smile, and I swallowed my pills thinking all the pain in the world was worth it if the two of them got back together again.

I slept most of that day and the next one too. Mom wanted me to stay in bed, so she kept the air conditioner blasting and piled blankets on top of me. It made me feel guilty hearing the hum of the air-conditioning motor, like all the nice cool air through the vents was actually dollars flying out of my parents' bank account.

Allie called, but my mom wouldn't let me have my phone. "You need to rest," she said. We didn't get to talk until Monday afternoon, when my mom finally gave it back to me. There were a couple of messages from Tim, too—he must have got the number from Allie. He wanted to check up on me. Southern guys are polite that way.

When Allie and I finally spoke, I told her I was sorry we'd left her at the party.

"Oh, don't worry about that," she said. "I got a ride with some girls." Then she told me all the details I didn't know about when I got burned, and she asked me all about my hand, and when I'd be back at school. I told her maybe Thursday, because by then I wouldn't need the pain medication.

"But I have to wear this bandage for three entire *months*! You know what that means? No guitar lessons. And what if it keeps me from getting a part in the play?" I felt a rush of anger, and now, thanks to Allie, I knew who it was directed toward: Caroline Jones.

"Oh, I found out for you," Allie said. "Auditions are next Monday, so you're okay. The play's called *Finian's Rainbow*."

Well, that was good. I felt relieved that at least I'd be able to try out. I wanted so badly to be up on that stage.

Allie told me all about cheerleading tryouts, which she'd just gotten back from. "I hope you'll be back on Friday," she said. "They're posting the team, and I need you for moral support. What if I don't make it?"

"You'll make it," I said. I wasn't just being nice telling her this. Other than her parents not letting her model, I could hardly remember a single instance of Allie not getting something she really wanted. Plus, she used to be so good at gymnastics. When I'd asked her how tryouts went, she didn't put herself down at all, just said that she thought they went pretty well.

Then she took a deep breath. "So tell me," she said, "what about the ride with Tim?"

"You mean to the hospital? There's not a whole lot to tell.

He drove fast. My hand killed like you wouldn't believe. That's pretty much the whole story."

"I about died when he took his shirt off," Allie said.

"He's a quick thinker." I don't know why, but I felt kind of protective of Tim. Like he'd been so good to me it didn't feel right to gossip about him, even if the gossip was saying he looked good without his shirt.

Allie let out a little breath, almost like she'd been holding it, and said, "I can't believe that on top of being so hot, he's smart and nice, too. I like him so much, Wren. Can you believe what a hero he was after you fell? I almost wished it was me that burned my hand."

Now that might sound ridiculous to you, but one of the things I loved about Allie was that she would come out and say something like that. It's what I said before, about just admitting you're jealous, even over something like a major second-degree burn.

"You sure won't wish that when you see the mitt I have to wear for the next three months," I told her, then made a joke about how at least I wouldn't have to do so much manure shoveling for a while.

My mom came in and told me to hang up so I could get some rest. After I said good-bye to Allie, Mom sat down on my bed, and I told her the name of the school play. She laughed and said her high school had done that play too.

"Did you have a part?" I asked her.

"I was in the chorus. But I remember the songs. I can teach you."

She sang this real pretty song called "How Are Things in Glocca Morra?" Mom has a great singing voice. There were some high parts, so I felt pretty glad to have extra days at home to practice.

By Tuesday afternoon I felt well enough to get up and walk around a bit. I watched a couple of movies downstairs and ate lunch in the kitchen. I wanted to go out to the barn and sit in the stall with Pandora, but Mom said it was too soon and the barn was too dirty. It was true my hand still hurt, but my body didn't feel quite so connected to it anymore. So I resigned myself to lying out front in the hammock reading *Invisible Man* for English. And you will never guess who came pedaling up our driveway, as if there not only wasn't an alligator in our river, but like he'd done it a hundred times before. Tim Greenlaw.

Mom was out at the barn with Daisy, so luckily, he did not have to contend with the Hellhound. I didn't get out of the hammock, just shaded my eyes with my book and watched Tim lay his bike in the grass. As he walked over to me, his hands in his pockets and his hair flopping in his eyes, I felt bad that he was turning up at *my* house when Allie liked him so much. At the same time I felt this happy little flutter in my gut.

"Hey," Tim said. He reached out and gave the hammock a gentle push. I wished I was wearing something nicer than old pajama shorts and a UNC T-shirt.

"Hey," I said.

"How's your hand?"

I held it up, the white bandage looking so big and round you could have drawn a map of the world on it. "I'm sorry I didn't call you back," I said. "My parents have been rationing phone time so I can rest up."

Mom chose this exact moment to return from the barn. When Daisy saw Tim, she started barking like crazy and charged at us. Tim froze and put his hands up in the air like a SWAT team had just drawn their rifles on him.

My mother came running up to grab Daisy's collar. "I'm sorry," she said to Tim, and then she scolded Daisy. Daisy lowered her barking to a rumbling growl, but she didn't look convinced. Neither did Tim. All the blood had drained from his face.

"Dang," he said, as Mom dragged Daisy away.

"I know," I said. "She saves us all kinds of money on burglar alarms." Tim laughed, but he still looked uneasy.

Mom slammed Daisy into the house and came on back to us. Tim recovered enough to say, "Hello, Mrs. Piner."

"Hello," Mom said. She looked a little confused, so I told her that he was the one who'd driven me to the hospital.

"You?" Mom said to Tim, like I wasn't a completely reliable

source of information. "You drove Wren to the hospital?"

"Yes, ma'am," Tim said.

Mom threw her arms around him. She had to stand on her tippy toes to do this, and I could see Tim smiling as he hugged her back with one arm. My mother is not the most domestic person in the world, but the day before she had made a strawberry rhubarb crumble on account of my injury. She went inside to warm some up, and pretty soon Tim and I were sitting at the outside table under the live oak, eating warm crumble with vanilla ice cream on top while Daisy barked her head off in the kitchen. By now she sounded less protective, and more insulted that she couldn't join us.

"Caroline Jones asked me for your number," Tim said. "She feels terrible."

I told Tim it wasn't Caroline's fault, even though it absolutely was. "You can give her my number if you want," I said. "But she doesn't need to call. I'm not mad at her." Of course this last bit wasn't entirely true, but I thought it made me sound like a nicer person. Funny how sometimes pretending can lead to really feeling a particular way, because as soon as I said it, I started to feel less mad. It'd been an accident, after all.

"She'll feel better when I tell her that," he said. He sounded so caring it made me wonder if they'd gotten back together.

Tim asked a lot of polite questions about our farm and the horses. I pointed out Pandora, who was grazing in the west field, along with my mom's favorite horse, Sombrero. I wanted to invite Tim back for a ride, but then I thought of Allie, and anyway it would probably be a long time before my mom would let me. We talked about the play, and the different parts. Tim said he wanted to play the leprechaun.

"You'd be an awful tall leprechaun," I said. As soon as the words were out of my mouth, I hoped they didn't sound like flirting. "Do you feel like you'll miss football?" I added quickly.

"Yeah," he said. "I wish I could do both. My dad's disappointed, but truthfully, my mom never liked my playing much. She always worried I'd crack my head or injure my spine."

"She sounds like my mother," I said. It was so easy to talk to Tim I decided I had nothing to feel guilty about, Allie-wise. Around Ry, for example, I always found myself all nervous and tongue-tied. The fact that I didn't feel this way around Tim clearly meant I had no crush on him whatsoever.

But still, as I waved good-bye and told him to watch out for our alligator as he biked down the road, I found myself feeling sad that he was leaving. I decided it would be better if I didn't mention his visit to Allie. She had enough on her mind worrying about cheerleading.

Four

My mother, on the other hand, strongly disagreed with not telling Allie about Tim visiting. I had to mention it because Allie came to sleep over on Thursday night so we could go to school together on Friday. My mother didn't want me to go to school at all, but I couldn't let Allie find out about cheerleading without me. She would need someone to celebrate with her, and before that she would need someone to calm her nerves. So as Mom and I sat out on the front stoop waiting for Allie's mom to drop her off, I said, "You know that guy who came by the other day?"

"Tim?" Mom said. She has an excellent memory for names.

"Uh-huh," I said. "Could you please not say anything about him when Allie's here?"

Mom gave me one of her sharp looks. "Wren," she said, "what's this about?" That's Mom—she always gets right to the point.

I sighed. "It's not *about* anything," I said. "Allie likes him, that's all, and it might make her feel bad if she knew he came by to see me."

"She'll feel worse if she finds out you're keeping things from her."

"It's not a big deal, Mom."

As these words came out of my mouth, they sounded a little like a lie. Because would you like to know how many times a handsome boy has bicycled up the driveway to visit me? Zero times, that's how many. Until Tim Greenlaw. Which felt just the teensiest bit like a big deal, all by itself.

But apparently I'd convinced my mother, even if I hadn't convinced myself. "Then why not tell Allie about it?" she pressed. She loves her moral high horse.

"I will eventually," I said. "But Allie's not quite herself lately. You know how her parents won't let her model. And then the beginning of school . . . I don't think it's exactly what she expected."

Mom studied my face carefully. Then she smiled a little. "Allie was born in the wrong place, wasn't she? She'd probably do better where I grew up. Allie's awfully exotic for Williamsport."

"Part giraffe," I said, and she smiled.

"It's hard being different in high school," Mom said. "It's the only time in your life when being normal really matters."

"Am I normal?"

Mom looked at me and frowned, but it was a frown that had a good deal of smile to it. "You can pass for normal," she said. "But you're not really. Thank goodness."

"Well, does that mean I was born in the wrong place too?"

My mother reached out and pushed a strand of hair off my forehead. "I don't think there could be a wrong place for you, Wren. You've always been comfortable in your own skin. And I hope you always will be."

I thought I'd rather be comfortable in Allie's skin but didn't get a chance to say so because the Hacketts' car came rumbling up our driveway. By this time I didn't have to ask Mom if she'd say anything about Tim. I knew I had converted her to my way of thinking.

That night in my room, Allie told me she'd had a secret talk with her grandmother who lives in New York. "She says that I can come live with her after I finish high school," Allie said, "and she'll help me try to be a model."

"What about college?" I said.

Allie flopped back on my bed and let out an exasperated sigh. "You sound like my mom," she said. "They have colleges in New York, you know. But Grandma said maybe I could take a year off and live with her, and just try out for things. Then if it doesn't work out, I can go to college later."

I decided not to say anything about how Allie's parents

would strangle her grandmother if they knew about that conversation. The two of them weren't adjunct instructors, like my dad, but bona fide, tenured PhDs. As you can imagine, education was pretty important to them. Both of them were pretty normal-looking. Allie's older brother was normal-looking too, and so was her little sister. Allie must have just lucked into some wild-card gorgeous gene.

"Maybe you can come to New York too," she said.

"Oh, sure," I said, and laughed. I had been to New York twice, and no modeling scout ever handed me a business card. The most exciting thing that happened was accidentally eating one of those tiny red peppers at a restaurant in Chinatown. It was so hot that I blacked out. One minute my teeth crunched into it, and the next thing I knew I was standing on the curb with Dad holding my head while I puked into the gutter. I reminded Allie of this story and she laughed too.

The next day at school it was like the alligator all over again. From the moment Allie and I stepped onto the school bus: CELEBRITY. Everyone knew about the accident and wanted to hear my version of events. They wanted to hear how bad my hand hurt, and how long I'd have to wear the bandage. When did Tim finally get a shirt at the hospital? Was I just *so* mad at Caroline Jones? At school Allie stood off to the side in her latest out-of-character, fully planned outfit, holding both our backpacks and listening. It may have been my imagination, but I thought she looked relieved when we had to say good-bye and head off to first period.

Later, on my way to lunch, I saw Caroline Jones for the first time. Honestly, I wouldn't have known it was her, since I'd only seen her in the dark, and so much had been happening. In calm daylight she was extremely pretty and grown-up-looking, with long brown hair and carrying herself like she was balancing an invisible book on her head. That morning someone told me that she was a dancer, which, when you think about it, was kind of ironic. My one experience with her had not been very graceful.

She glided right up to me, her face all quivery. "I can't tell you how sorry I am about your hand, Wren," she said. "Does it still hurt?"

"Not as much anymore," I said. "I'm taking Ibuprofen instead of the hard stuff. I just have to keep it covered and it'll be fine."

"Is it going to scar?" She looked really worried, staring at my bandaged hand, and so nice that it would've taken all my might to stay mad at her. At this point we were walking into the cafeteria. So far one of my least favorite things about Williamsport High was walking into that big cafeteria and not knowing where to sit. I told Caroline how James had said some of the lines on my hand might be gone once it healed. "So no more palm readers for me," I said.

"I'm so sorry, Wren," Caroline said. Wow, I'd only been joking. She sounded like she might cry.

"Hey," I said. "Except for the bottom of your foot, can you think of a better place for a scar?"

Finally Caroline smiled. "I guess not," she said. "But you let me know if there's anything I can do for you, okay?" And then she disappeared into the crowd, leaving me standing there with no place to go. Luckily, at that moment my eyes fell on Tim, sitting alone at a table and staring intently at a white piece of paper.

"Is this seat taken?" I said, pulling out the chair across from him. He looked up like I'd startled him, and I plopped down even though he didn't say anything. "What are you reading?" I asked.

He pushed the paper over to me. "It's an e-mail from my church," he said. "I printed it out in the library because there was a line for the computer."

It seemed kind of weird that he'd print it out instead of just saving it for later, or even deleting it. What could a church have to say that was so important? Truthfully, I wasn't especially interested in his e-mail, but I looked at it to be polite.

Maybe Tim could tell I was hardly reading it, because he said, "Our pastor's all mad because the national branch of our church voted to let gay people be ministers."

"What's wrong with that?"

Tim shrugged. "I guess he doesn't like gay people."

At almost this exact moment, Devon appeared at our table with Allie by his side. They joined us. "Gay people?" Devon said. "As in *homosexuals?*" He said the word like it was the funniest and stupidest thing you could say. He said, "Tim, we're trying to eat here," and then took a bite of his cafeteria burger.

Allie and I looked at each other. She was as uncomfortable as I was, but the glance she gave me was the same as the other night—pleading with me not to say anything. But I just couldn't let Devon's joke slide.

So I said, "I don't get it. Why can't you talk about gay people and eat at the same time?"

Tim reached out and took the paper away from me. He folded it up real neat and slid it into his backpack. Devon looked at me like I'd said I didn't know two plus two equaled four. Then he said, "Well, excuse me, Miss Politically Correct."

"It's got nothing to do with politics," I said. "It's about people."

"Yeah, people." He half laughed. "Like that poofter over there."

I turned my head to where he was pointing. Allie said, "Oh. Jesse Gill."

Jesse Gill had gone to Cutty River with us through middle school. He had pink streaks in his hair and wore a black T-shirt. He was also sitting all by himself. Allie waved at him, but he didn't seem to see her. Devon took another bite of his burger. It was weird—even though he was saying really mean things, his tone and expression were so lighthearted and friendly that it wasn't hard for me to argue with him.

"Jesse?" I said to Devon. "I know Jesse. But I don't know if he's gay or not, and neither do you." Truthfully, I was pretty sure Jesse was gay, but no way would I say that to Devon. "Even if he is, what do you care?"

Devon didn't get a chance to answer, because a couple of girls came over to the table to tell Allie that cheerleader results hadn't been posted yet but would be later that afternoon. I watched Allie talking to them, looking all smiley and energetic, and I thought how much happier she'd be once she was on the squad. I hoped she wouldn't forget all about me.

The girls moved on to another table, and we all went back to eating. Nobody much felt like reviving our previous conversation, though Devon kind of smiled at me like he didn't have any hard feelings. As if I was the one who'd said something offensive! I hoped Tim didn't think like Devon. I kind of worried he did, because he hadn't had a chance to tell me how he felt about that e-mail from his church. But he sat there looking at me, real thoughtful, in a way that made my stomach give one of those happy little

flutters. And it dawned on me that I had barely thought of
Ry once since I burned my hand.

As we walked over to the gym to see the cheerleading roster,
Allie said maybe I should be a little quieter about my opin-
ions. "Look, Wren, don't take this the wrong way, 'cause I
always like how you're so confident and everything. But you
don't have to say every little thing that comes into your head.
I mean, you don't want to embarrass anyone."

"Who did I embarrass?"

"I think you embarrassed the guys," she said. "You know
how they can be weird about . . . homosexuality." She pro-
nounced the word like it had eighteen syllables. She sounded
like she was thirty years old, and I told her so. Allie laughed.

Ahead of us a group of girls gathered all around a list
that was posted on the bulletin board outside the gym. Some
of them were already crying, others were high-fiving and
hugging. Allie gave me her backpack, then moved sideways
through the crowd. I stood there, waiting for her to come
back so we could high-five and hug too. Instead she came
elbowing out of the crowd with this dazed look on her face.

"I'm not on the list," she said, like she couldn't believe it.
"I didn't make the squad."

"What?" I said. "No. That couldn't be right." I left her
standing there to elbow *my* way through the crowd. Very
carefully, I ran my finger down the list, certain she had

somehow missed her name. I did it twice before I finally had to admit she was right: Her name wasn't there. It wasn't even on the list of alternates. Allie had not made the cheerleading squad.

"I can't believe it," she said, when I got back to her. I could tell she'd had a hope that I would find her name where she hadn't. "I just can't believe it." Her eyes started filling with tears.

"Maybe they only let juniors and seniors on," I said. She turned to walk out of the gym, and I followed her. "Maybe they wanted to make sure and give the older girls a chance, so they didn't choose any freshmen or sophomores."

"They did let sophomores on, and freshmen, too," Allie said. "I saw the names of two girls who I know are freshmen, and three sophomores."

"Well," I said. "That's not very many." Probably a lot more than five underclassmen had tried out. "Maybe for most girls, they wait till they're a little older." At this point we were walking across the lawn toward the bleachers by the baseball field.

"I know why they didn't choose me," Allie said, suddenly sounding ferocious. "It's because I'm so damn tall."

I don't know anything about cheerleading, but in that moment it struck me that Allie might be right. Maybe the coach thought it would look weird with her towering over all the other girls. Plus, didn't they have to pick each other up all the time?

"I'm too tall," Allie said furiously. "I'm too tall to be a cheerleader, and too tall for Tim to like me. I'm a freak. The only thing I'm right for is modeling, and I can't even do that." She burst into tears and sat down on the bottom bleacher.

"That's totally wrong if it's about height," I said, sitting next to her. "That's discrimination. We should talk to the coach about this."

"Don't," Allie said. "Don't you dare."

We sat there for a while, Allie crying and me not knowing what else I could say. I felt just terrible. Cheerleading was the whole reason she'd wanted to leave Cutty River School. I wondered if the same thing would happen to me and I wouldn't get a part in the play. I decided that if it did, I would work even harder and try out again for the next one. I started to tell Allie she should do the same thing, but before I got a chance she said, "And don't you tell me I can try out again next year. I am never trying out for anything again. Never."

I knew she'd feel differently next year, so I just let her cry a little bit more, and then I said, "Well, and anyway, who says Tim doesn't like you? Maybe he does."

At this she wiped her eyes and looked straight at me. "It doesn't seem like he likes me," she said. "It seems like he likes *you*."

"We're just friends," I assured her, but in that moment

I got a distinct hand-in-the-cookie-jar feeling, and hoped I didn't sound as guilty as I felt. "Buddies."

"Yeah?" she said. "So maybe you should ask him if he likes me."

I thought about this for a moment, trying to imagine how the conversation might go. Mostly I worried he might say he didn't. I sure didn't want to be the bearer of *that* news. And much as I hated to admit it, the way I'd started to feel meant I didn't particularly like the idea of him telling me he *did* like her, either. So I said, "Give me a week or two to get more comfortable."

"Okay," she said. I could almost hear her thinking that she might not have made the cheerleading squad, but at least she still had a chance at being Tim Greenlaw's girlfriend.

Five

Allie and her family came over to watch the alligator get removed from our river. Dad made it clear he was against this process. He kept telling us about an ornithologist he knew in Florida who had an American crocodile living in his driveway. The man traveled a lot, and people would ask him if he worried about leaving his wife alone in the house with that crocodile lying under the porch stairs. "Are you kidding?" the man would say. "She's the safest woman in Florida. Who's going to break into the house with that crocodile standing guard?"

"We've got Daisy," Mom said. "We don't need a crocodile. Or an alligator."

Dad ignored this and went on to say how somebody built a fancy trophy home next door to his friend, with a big pool, and then got upset when the crocodile started sunning itself on the dry deck. Three times they tried to move the crocodile to an island south of there, but every spring, guess who was back sunning himself by the fancy pool?

If Dad was trying to talk us out of removing the alligator, he only doubly convinced me to never go anywhere near the river ever again, because now I knew the alligator might come back. And Mom said she had enough to worry about without adding a seven-foot reptile to the equation. So on Saturday afternoon Mom, Dad, and me, plus Allie and her mother and little sister Sylvie, all stood in our driveway. Allie's brother was away at college and her father was in his office grading papers, which seems like exactly where he's been every minute of his life. The same cameraman from the local news came by, along with one of their anchors. The cameraman made a joke about the bandage on my hand. "Did the gator get it?" he said.

The cameraman was kind of cute, and I could tell Allie was annoyed he was paying attention to me instead of her. You know, I sometimes think being so pretty works against Allie. The cameraman could kid with me and it just seemed like razzing a teenager. But if he'd paid attention to Allie, it could have been taken the wrong way. I decided I would tell her that later; that'd make her feel better.

Although Dad was against the whole thing, he dressed in his forest service uniform so the alligator removal team would let him help. I had to admit the removal almost made me wish we'd just left the poor thing alone. They fished him out of there with these long white poles that had hooks on the end, while Sylvie kept yelling, "Don't hurt him!" The alligator barely struggled, just opened his mouth real wide. When they hauled him out of the river, one of the men sat right on his back.

As they loaded the alligator into the back of their truck, I felt so sad and disappointed. I also felt guilty. Probably that alligator had been in the river all summer, and it had never bothered a soul. All those times I'd gone swimming it never even thought about eating me. Now it was getting carted off to someplace far from home, who knew where, just because I wasn't brave enough to live nearby it.

Once the alligator was loaded, the main removal guy turned to wave at us. "Don't you worry, little lady," he said to Sylvie. "We didn't hurt that gator one bit."

Watching them drive away, I couldn't help feeling that the alligator would probably not agree.

That afternoon Allie's mom drove Allie and me downtown so we could have lunch and walk around. On the drive nobody said anything about cheerleading tryouts, which surprised me a little.

"I didn't tell her," Allie explained as we headed over to the music store. "She'll try to be comforting, but I'll be able to tell she's happy about it. So I told her they weren't posting it till Monday. I wish they could understand," she added, "that just because a thing is not important to them doesn't mean it's not important."

The door on the music store jingled as we walked in. My mother had already called Ry to tell him I wouldn't be taking lessons for a while, but I wanted to use this opportunity to show him my bandage and tell him to watch for me on the news that night. Allie saw him before I did. She gave a little gasp and reached out to grab my elbow.

There was Ry, all right. He stood over by the ukuleles, talking to a girl who was clearly not just a friend. They were smiling at each other with particularly shiny eyes, and all the while they were talking they had their hands twined together. I stepped back, but then Allie cleared her throat. I wished she hadn't of. I just wanted to get out of there. Ry looked over at us like he'd been woken out of a trance. It took him a couple of seconds to even remember who I was.

"Oh, hey, Wren," he said. He let go of the girl's hand, which took some doing since their fingers were so tangled up together. "How's your wrist?"

"It's my hand," I said. I held up my bandage to show him. "It's real bad. I probably won't ever play guitar again."

"Ever?" he said. "Your mom said you could start again this winter."

"No," I said. I felt like an idiot, and a little kid, but I couldn't stop myself. I was so close to crying. "I am never going to play guitar again."

Then I turned around and ran out of the store, Allie right behind. It was dramatic, and I didn't bother turning around to see the looks on Ry's and his girlfriend's faces. I could imagine well enough anyway. They would look totally confused, and then after a minute they would start laughing about another stupid little girl in love with Ry. Probably three of us a day run out of that music store in tears.

"Aw, Wren, that sucks," Allie said, as we sat down to eat slices of pizza at the Good Life. "I can just imagine how I'd feel, if I saw Tim like that with another girl. And just when things were going so well for you."

"Allie," I said. "My river is infested with reptiles and I nearly burned my hand off in a bonfire." At the same time I said this I knew exactly what she meant. These two unfortunate occurrences had led to all sorts of attention and new friends. Funny how life can be that way. For example, after the initial shock, I found myself not feeling especially sad about Ry. Sure, I was embarrassed about how I left the music shop. "But truthfully," I told Allie, "what did I expect would happen? I'm sixteen. Ry's, like, twentysomething."

"He could be arrested," Allie agreed. "And anyway, he's got snaggly teeth."

I shrugged. I thought Ry's teeth gave him character, but I didn't feel like arguing.

"Maybe now you can have a boyfriend your own age,"

Allie said. "I can go out with Tim and you can go out with Devon."

Devon? Huh. He might act nice, but by now I felt pretty sure he *wasn't* so nice. The more I thought about it, the more I knew I wouldn't go out with him if you paid me a million dollars. I would've expected Allie to realize this, but the idea made her so happy that I didn't argue.

Allie's mom drove me home, and instead of heading inside I snuck out to the barn. Even though I wasn't cleared to ride yet, I could still climb up on Pandora's back. It's something I've always liked to do to calm myself down—just climb on up, and then lie back with my head on her rump, staring up at the pine-board ceiling and taking in the scent of clean hay and straw.

Tryouts for *Finian's Rainbow* were on Monday after school. My mom and I had been practicing singing "How Are Things in Glocca Morra?" all the past week and I felt pretty good, though she kept warning me about how a sophomore probably wouldn't get to play Sharon. That was her nice way of saying that no matter how well I sang, I looked way too young to play the lead. Unlike Tim Greenlaw. I wondered if he could really sing, and what part he'd get. I thought about what happened with Allie and cheerleading and reminded myself not to get my hopes up. Allie had finally broken down and told her parents that she hadn't made the squad. She was so sad about it that her mother called up the coach. According to her mom, it was all pretty cut-and-dried. Two hundred girls had tried out for twenty spots, plus five alternates. The coach said Allie should try again next year, because she was real good. "Just not good enough," Allie had told me. I knew full well the same thing could happen to me with the play.

Williamsport High built their state-of-the-art theater before the economy fell apart, and it's just as nice as Raphael Hall, which is the place downtown where they give concerts. In fact, it's even nicer than Raphael Hall, because it's all updated with the most modern equipment and decor. For the auditions they had us all wait out in the lobby, I guess so people couldn't make fun of the ones who didn't perform well. It was so crowded that I had to sit on the floor. I saw Tim was already there, hanging out with a couple of older kids over on the other side of the room.

"Hi, Wren," a voice above me said. I looked up and saw Jesse Gill standing there. I moved my backpack so he could sit next to me.

"You trying out?" I asked stupidly.

"Yeah," he said. "It's the whole reason I came here, you know, and last year I didn't get a part in the fall play or the spring. I really hope I get in this year." His voice sounded tired. It made me wonder if people had been teasing him, but I didn't feel comfortable asking. Jesse and I had known each other for a long time, but we'd never hung out much.

Almost right away they called Jesse's name. "Break a leg," I told him as he headed in. I really hoped he'd get a part, he looked so sad and lonesome.

By the time a lady poked her head through the door and called, "Wren Piner," the lobby was half-empty. Everyone left looked over to see who was going next, so I waved a little as I scrambled to my feet. My mother likes to tell this story about how when I was five or six I heard her telling someone she suffered from terrible stage fright, and I said, "I am not related to your stage fright." In this instance, though, I had to admit I felt nervous.

There were three people sitting in the front row holding clipboards. One of them, a woman, said, "Wren?"

"Yes, ma'am."

"What are you going to sing for us?"

I told her "How Are Things in Glocca Morra?" and she said, "Oh, good. Victor sure knows how to play that, don't you, Victor?"

He played the first couple of notes, and then I joined in. I did it just the way Mom and I had practiced, real quiet on the first few lines ("I hear a bird"), and then belting it out on the first "Glocca Morra." They let me sing the whole entire song, and when I finished, everyone sat real quiet.

Finally the main woman said, "It says here you're a sopho-more. Is that correct?"

"Yes, ma'am."

"Well, Wren, you sing well. Very well."

"Thank you, ma'am."

"But I need to tell you, we usually cast the older students in lead roles."

What was I supposed to say to that? Okay? It didn't seem particularly okay. I thought about telling her I was sixteen, but I figured the policy was to give everyone a fair chance, and even if I was eighteen, I had three years here to be in plays. She asked some more questions about my hand—what had happened and when the bandage was coming off. Then Victor handed me a script, and the woman—by now I'd found out her name was Ms. Winters—read a page or so with me. She let me read the role of Sharon, even though she'd as good as told me I'd never get that part.

When I came out of the audition, Tim was standing by the door, waiting for me. "How did it go?" he asked.

I felt kind of confused about how it had gone, and I told Tim so. "Well," he said, "you'll find out on Wednesday. Want to wait with me? You can come in and hear me sing." I'd noticed that a couple of people brought their friends in to hear their audition. "We have to take the late bus, anyway," he added.

So that's how I ended up back in the auditorium, listening

to Tim sing. He didn't sing a song from the play. Instead he sang this Ben Harper song called "I Believe in a Better Way." I thought he was really good, and when he finished, Ms. Winters did not warn him not to expect a good role. She just said, "That was excellent, Tim. I'm glad you found the time for us this year."

Tim smiled, and then read some pages of the script with her. He did an Irish accent and everything, and I counted five times that he made the people watching laugh, including the piano player. Sitting in the back row watching all this, with no one watching me, I wondered what it would be like to let myself have a crush on Tim now that Ry was out of the picture. Obviously that still left Allie as an obstacle, but as I told you, sometimes I am a terrible friend. A miserable friend.

Sitting there, I thought about what it would be like if I was Tim's girlfriend. Probably he would save me a seat every day on the bus. And I'd never have to worry about where to sit in the cafeteria, because I could always sit with him. Maybe he'd hold my hand when we walked down the hall. I'd give him a picture of myself to hang up in his locker. Of course it was totally 100 percent disloyal of me to think all these things—the very things my best friend in the whole world might be thinking right at that very moment. But I couldn't help myself, and I'd gone this far, so I just kept going.

didn't even go see it right after it was posted, because I didn't want to have to stand in a crowd the way Allie had done for cheerleading. Instead, on Wednesday afternoon I skipped the early bus and waited till everyone had either gone home or headed off to their after-school activity. Just as I hoped, the auditorium was empty. I walked over to the list and ran my finger down to find Sharon. Sure enough, another girl's name was listed.

Next, I skipped straight to the chorus. My name wasn't there. I couldn't believe it. I didn't make the play at all! Allie and I might just as well have stayed at Cutty River.

I took a deep breath and raised one of my good fingers to the top of the list. Very carefully and slowly I ran it down the piece of paper until it stopped—right there in black and white—on my name. Wren Piner.

I walked over to the couch and sat down to call my mother. I tried not to let my voice sound too excited. "I got a part," I told her. "I'm a 'Necessity' girl. There are three of them. I don't even know what that means."

"Wren, that's a great part!" Mom said. "In my production just one girl sang it, but they must be staging it as a trio. It's a great song, a real showstopper. That's wonderful, Wren; I'm so proud of you." She told me to hang on, went to her computer, and looked it up on YouTube, then held up the phone so I could hear it. Those singers were really belting it out to the rafters.

When the bandage came off my hand, I could take Tim
riding at the farm. I'd ride Pandora, of course, and if he
didn't have much experience he could ride Brutus, who
used to be one of our most uneasy horses but now was so old
even Allie's sister Sylvie could ride him. Tim and I would
ride across the fields at the farm, and we could ride down
the Old Farthing Road. Maybe we could even sneak and
camp out there together. Now that the alligator was gone,
we could wade in the river. And Tim could kiss me.

Allie called me later that day to see how tryouts went. When
I heard her voice I felt like a total rat, almost as if I hadn't
just imagined kissing Tim but had actually done it. I shook
that thought out of my head and told her I did well but the
teacher told me I probably wouldn't get a part. Really Ms.
Winters had said I probably wouldn't get a *lead* part, but I
found myself adjusting this information.

"Oh my God, we're cursed!" Allie said.

In my opinion she sounded a little too happy about it,
but I forgave her on account of my earlier treacherous
thoughts. And actions. For example, I did not tell her that
I watched Tim try out, or that he and I rode home together
on the late bus.

Here's another bad thing I did: I told Allie they were
posting the cast on Friday. Don't ask me why; I just felt
like I needed to be by myself when I looked at the list. I

"What do you think, Wren? Isn't it a great song?"

"It really is," I said.

Mom was so excited she drove in from Leeville to take me out for ice cream. I didn't tell her that the boy who'd rescued me from the fire would also be playing her favorite part: Og the leprechaun.

Six

On Friday afternoon we had our first rehearsal. Tim had a few big numbers, and I sat watching him with another guy who usually played football, Tyler Caldwell. At one point in the play this evil, racist senator gets turned into an African-American man, and Tyler was playing him after the transformation. Tyler agreed that Tim sang great, but still couldn't understand why anyone would voluntarily give up football to be a leprechaun. Tyler himself had some kind of knee injury, which was the only reason he was sitting out this season.

The role of Og was very silly and cute, and the way Tim acted him out was just hilarious. Sitting next to Tyler, watching Tim up onstage, I felt this longing in my gut that I knew made me nothing but a big fat traitor.

That longing also made it extremely fun to ride home on the late bus with Tim. What else could I do, anyway?

Tell him he couldn't sit next to me? Because that's exactly what he did—he got onto the bus and beelined right for the seat beside me. I was starting to agree with Allie's earlier suspicions. It seemed like maybe Tim liked me, though that seemed pretty crazy. Maybe he hadn't figured out Allie had a crush on him.

When the bus stopped at the end of my driveway, he said, "Hey, can I come up and see your horses?"

I sure loved the idea of spending more time with Tim, but I had to think about this for a moment. Allie was already ticked at me for lying about when the play results were posted, and even though she'd *never* admit it, I was pretty sure she was also mad at me for getting a part when she hadn't made cheerleading. Plus, she looked at me funny anytime Tim came near. So I knew I should make an excuse. A good friend would, wouldn't she? But there was Tim, waiting for me to answer, and out of my mouth came, "Sure. Do you like horses?"

"Yeah," he said. "I wanted one when I was a kid, but we didn't have the money for it."

"My parents don't have the money for it either," I said.

Tim laughed like he didn't believe me. Everyone always thinks we're rich because of our horses and property. Little do they know. But if Tim needed any convincing as to our nonwealth, he sure got it when we reached the top of the driveway. Something I hadn't seen in a long while, an unfamiliar horse trailer, was parked in front of the house. Daisy came running up to greet me and to menace Tim, but even over her barking we could hear Dad loud and clear.

"You've got no business bringing him here," Dad was yelling at my mother. He doesn't get mad too often, but when he does, look out. I could feel my face go red, and on top of everything else I thought that if only I were a more loyal friend, I would be witnessing this all alone instead of with Tim standing beside me.

"Please," Mom said, her voice full of tears. The man who must have brought the horse stood off to the side with his arms crossed, staring down at the ground like he wished he were anyplace else in the world. I guess the horse was lame, because its back leg was bandaged and Dad was yelling about vet bills.

"You think you're doing this animal a favor," he finished, "but it's going to end up out on the street along with the rest of us!"

I figured Tim had heard enough. I touched his elbow and said, "Come on."

We walked across our west field toward the barn. Tim didn't say anything and neither did I. When we got to the barn, I brought him straight over to Pandora. She looked over her stall door all calm and at home, like she couldn't imagine ever living anywhere else. Last year Mom had gotten an adoption offer for her and turned it down. "I won't give away Wren's favorite horse," Mom had told Dad, by way of argument. She had said the same thing when someone wanted to adopt Sombrero, even though he was actually *her* favorite horse, which Dad knew as well as I did. The way Mom loved her horses was one of the things he loved best about her, and I figured we must be in deep trouble for him to be hollering about it.

Pandora snuffled her nose at my pocket. Usually I would have brought a sugar cube or carrot for her. "Sorry, girl," I said, and ran my good palm over the tiny white mark between her eyes, then pressed my nose into the space between her nostrils, the softest thing in the whole wide world.

Tim petted Pandora's neck. "She's beautiful," he said. I could tell he didn't plan on saying a word about what we'd just seen, and I felt grateful for that.

"All the horses are beautiful," I said. "They're bred to be fast and strong and beautiful, and people just want to throw them away when they can't make money anymore, or if they don't perform the way they wanted them to. If it weren't for my mom, these horses would be bottles of Elmer's Glue or cans of Alpo. She's not being irresponsible. She just wants to save them."

Tim didn't say anything. He just kept petting Pandora's neck in a way that showed he wasn't used to horses at all. I introduced him to Brutus, and also Sombrero, whose back was kind of sweaty, with marks from a recent currycomb, so probably Mom had been riding him that afternoon. As we walked by the tack room, I noticed Dad had left one of his rifles leaning against the wall. This is the kind of thing that infuriates my mother, so I went in and took the key from her desk. "Mom won't let him keep these in the house," I told Tim as I put the rifle back in the gun case with the others. I had to hang it up one-handed on account of my bandages. Even though my hand had stopped hurting so bad, it made doing the most regular things just a little bit more difficult.

"Wow, look at all those rifles," Tim said. "My parents don't have any."

"Dad doesn't hunt," I said. "He just likes to shoot at targets that he sets up in the woods. And he says cleaning a gun always helps clear his mind."

We walked outside to see who was in the paddock, and I pointed out different horses. "That horse is named Birdie, but she used to be called Sunday Best. She ran the Kentucky Derby and won a bunch of other races, but then she got soft-tissue injuries and wound up here."

"Doesn't seem like a bad place to wind up," Tim said.

For some reason this made me feel like crying, so I tried to change the subject. "You sure were funny in rehearsal today," I said.

"You already told me that on the bus." He sounded so nice when he said this. Like he wanted to remind me he knew I was sad, and that was okay. "So," he said, turning things back to my life, the last place I wanted things to go. "Do you have any brothers or sisters?"

"No," I said. "It's just me. How about you?"

"Older sister. Kathy. She's at Duke."

We walked out a little bit to the top of the hill and sat down. It was a good view. To one side you could see our house, and the driveway, and various horses grazing. To the other side you could see Cutty River Landing, all those brick houses and their shiny pool. "Look," Tim said. "You can see my house from here."

"Really? You live at Cutty River Landing?" He tried to point out his house, but they all looked the same, so it was hard to see which one he meant. I tried to imagine what it would be like, living down there in one of those brick houses, with maybe just a dog or a cat, and all the bills paid so you never had to hear your parents fight.

Finally it hit me, that it was weird I hadn't said anything about my parents fighting. So I said, "Tim. I'm really sorry you had to see that before. With my mom and dad."

"That's okay," he said. "You should hear my parents sometimes."

Again, he sounded so nice. He *was* so nice, I found myself saying, "We're having some problems with money, if you couldn't tell. Hanging on to this place."

Tim put his hand on my shoulder for a minute. The weight of his palm there, and the weight of what I'd just said, pressed down on me in opposite ways, both of them so emotional I worried I'd start crying.

"Don't tell anyone," I said. "Okay? I don't want to talk to anyone about it just yet."

"I won't," Tim said. "You can trust me, Wren, I promise."

I lay back in the grass and Tim's hand dropped off me. He lay back too, and the two of us just stared up at the blue sky, wispy little white clouds floating up there above us. The worst of summer's heat had passed, and while it still felt warm, there was the tiniest little breeze moving things around. It was so pretty I could almost stop thinking about my parents fighting.

Tim pushed up on one elbow and looked down into my face. I looked back at him. His blond hair hung off his forehead, and I saw every single freckle, plus the flecks of green and gold in his blue eyes. I wondered if he was about to kiss me. Of course if he did, it would bring about all sorts of problems. But you know what? I didn't particularly care. My whole heart felt clutched up, beating hard. This boy might be about to kiss me, a boy I liked. I didn't even want to think about how much I liked him. If Tim kissed me, today would be the day of my first real kiss, and nothing else would matter, not even my parents having a big fight over a new horse and Dad saying we were all going to end up on the street.

Looking back on this moment, I believe that Tim really

was thinking about kissing me. He even leaned in a little closer so I could feel his breath on my face, soft, like he was trying to hold it. I thought about closing my eyes but I didn't, because I wanted to know what it looked like when a person kissed you on the lips.

But instead of kissing me, Tim said, "Wren, can I tell you something?"

"Sure," I said. It surprised me how disappointed I felt. My heart did not want to slow down. Tim pushed off his elbow and lay back down beside me. We went back to watching clouds again, long enough for me to wonder if he'd changed his mind, or fallen asleep.

Then he said, "Do you promise not to tell anyone?"

"Sure," I said. Tim had come to the right place. I am good at keeping secrets. But I had this sinking feeling that he was going to tell me he liked Allie.

But that's not what he said at all. In fact, when he did speak, I couldn't be sure I heard him right, because it sounded like, "I think I like guys."

"What?" I said.

"I think I like guys," he repeated. This time he sounded kind of sorry he'd said it.

"What do you mean, like them?"

"I think I'm gay. I mean, I know I am."

"How do you know?" I asked.

"I just do."

Now, this had never crossed my mind in regards to Tim—nothing about him was like what I thought about when I thought about a gay person—and yet it made perfect sense. I can't say why, exactly. But it was like a window shade being snapped up and letting the light in. Everything just lay out clear before me and fell into its proper place. Which doesn't at all mean that I wasn't let down. At the same time I felt kind of flattered, that he would share this big a secret with me.

I tried to think of what to say next, and asked if there were someone particular he liked, hoping it wouldn't be Devon.

"No," Tim said.

His voice sounded a tiny bit strained, like maybe he wished he hadn't said anything. Even though I felt like something truly wonderful had just been snatched away from me, I knew he had told me this as a friend. Because he trusted me, just like he said I could trust him. So I said, "Well, that's okay, Tim. I'm glad you told me." I turned my face to look at him, but he kept staring up at the clouds.

"I never told anyone before." His face looked sad.

I said, "I'm honored."

He turned toward me to see if I was kidding. I stared back at him, trying to look as sincere as I possibly could. This was the first time anyone had told me he was gay, so I didn't know the etiquette. All of a sudden Tim did what he hadn't done before: He kissed me. He grabbed my face and kissed me full on the lips, with his mouth closed, and then he kissed me again.

"I knew you would say that," he said. "I love you, Wren. I truly do."

I probably don't need to tell you that this moment did not match up with my previous fantasies of a first kiss, not to mention the first time a boy telling me he loved me. So I couldn't help it: I burst out laughing, and after a moment so did Tim. He got to his feet and held out his hand. I took it, and that's how we walked back down to the house— holding hands, the sun shining all around us.

Tim borrowed Dad's bike, and we rode over to his house at Cutty River Landing. I waved good-bye at the end of his driveway, then pedaled on home. Mom was waiting for me out front to remind me of all the afternoon chores I'd left undone. Dad's Jeep was gone. So was the horse trailer and, to my surprise, the horse. Never in my life had I known Dad to win an argument like that one. Mom's face looked red and puffy. I wondered where the horse had gone. I never had to think about that before, what happened to horses that Mom didn't save, because she always did—save them, that is.

I didn't have the heart to complain about anything, just walked out to the barn with her and set right into polishing tack. It was kind of awkward with my bandaged hand, but Mom just watched me without offering to help. She sat on top of her crowded little desk and said, "Tim seems really interested in you, Wren."

I naturally tensed up a little at this, but then decided Tim was a better topic of conversation than the horse that got sent away. "We're just friends, Mom," I said. I wished I could tell her the truth, but certainly didn't plan to break my promise to Tim, even though Mom wouldn't care about it one single bit, and she certainly wouldn't tell Devon Kelly, or anyone else at Williamsport High.

"Well," Mom said. "He seems very nice. Your grandfather would have called him the right sort."

For a second I stopped scrubbing the bit. I knew how much she missed her father whenever things got hard. "Mom," I said, giving up on my idea not to mention it. "I'm really sorry you couldn't keep the new horse."

A funny kind of look came into her eyes, one I'd never seen before. Almost like panic. It scared me a little. "That horse," Mom whispered. "That horse is the least of it."

I felt a terrible sort of emptiness open up in my stomach. For as long as I could remember, my parents had been scrambling and scraping to hold on to this place. But they always did hold on. I knew that two of Mom's biggest donors had lost a ton of money in the stock market, but somehow I thought that we'd still get by. Maybe I never thought life would get easy, but I never dreamed we'd truly lose the farm. Because how in the world could I ever live anywhere else? This place was *my* place, my home, as much as if I'd sprung from the tall grass by the river.

Mom must have seen the look on my face, because she said, "This isn't for you to worry about, Wren. Dad and I will take care of it. We'll find a way to work it out."

It took all my strength not to yell at her. *Not for me to worry about? Who was she kidding?* But then I noticed she seemed to have all these new lines around her mouth, but she also looked as sad as a little kid, young and old at the same time. My mother was the most softhearted person in the world. All she ever wanted to do was take care of things that couldn't take care of themselves.

"Mom," I said, wanting to give her a little gift, "I need to tell you something about Tim."

"What?" She blinked at me like she felt a little afraid of what I might say.

"He's playing Og," I said. "The leprechaun."

Mom smiled at this, but she didn't light up the way I hoped she would. Later on I called Allie, but she didn't answer the phone, so I just lay on my bed, staring at the ceiling and thinking about Tim. I remembered that flyer from his church, about gay ministers, and all the things I'd heard Devon say right in front of him. I wondered what Tim was doing, and if he felt weird about having told me. Hopefully he wasn't worried at all, or wishing he hadn't done it. Somehow I would find a way to let him know for sure that I would never give his secret away, not to anyone. He might have other things he needed to worry about, but that sure wasn't one of them.

When I got downstairs the next morning, my dad was waiting for me in the kitchen. He had his binoculars around his neck and a wide-brimmed hat on his head. Going-for-a-walk clothes. Sure enough he told me, "Go on up and change. You and me are going for a walk."

Sometimes Dad will take me for a walk on forest service land, but I guess today he felt like staying close to home. He told me to keep a lookout for a painted bunting, which he thought he'd heard out by the far pasture the other day. We walked across our back lawn and then into the woods that divided our property from Cutty River Landing.

"You know, Wren," Dad said, after we'd walked in silence awhile with no sign of the painted bunting. "That Tim fellow seems nice enough. But you're not old enough to date."

"Right," I said. "Except you know that I am."

Dad laughed. When a bird trilled from the top of a long-leaf pine and he looked at it through his binoculars, I knew he was going to ask me to identify it, so I went ahead and said, "Carolina wren."

"Good girl," he said, even though I'd known that one since I was five, seeing it was the bird he'd named me after.

I waited for him to say something like he usually did, about me being *his* Carolina wren, or else for him to say something more about Tim. In a weird way I kind of liked it that everyone, including my parents, thought that such a cool and handsome guy liked me. It made me feel special, even if it wasn't true. Even if what *was* true might change Tim from one of the most popular guys at school to an outcast like Jesse Gill. Which seemed so unfair, and I hoped again that Tim wasn't worried about me telling Allie, or anyone else.

Meanwhile Dad had apparently said all he meant to about Tim, as he switched the subject completely. "I guess I don't need to tell you, Wren. We're in a bit of trouble here." He put his binoculars down and sat on a log. A couple of greenheads buzzed around his hat, but he didn't even bother waving them away. He just started talking. He said a lot of things I already knew, like how donations to my mother's rescue efforts had pretty much dried up since the economy fell apart, and how Mom kept turning down offers to adopt horses even when they did come in, because she always wanted their homes to be just perfect.

"Not that any of this is her fault," he put in quickly. "She did a great job with this place for a long time. She couldn't have known what would happen." He started talking about how much money people had been losing in the last few years. And then he said that they hadn't wanted to tell me, but Mr. George Lee, one of Mom's biggest donors—the man who owned the Mercedes dealership—had committed suicide because his business went under.

"Not Mr. George Lee," I said. I couldn't believe it. Mr. Lee used to bring his kids by the farm to visit with the horses. His youngest daughter was just a few years older than me. Tears sprang to my eyes, thinking of her losing her father in such an awful way.

Dad must have seen how I was about to cry. He took a deep breath and said, "I'm sorry to have to tell you all this, Wren. But you need to know. Things are bad all over. And now the university's going through all kinds of cuts. They're not going to renew my contract. Already I was down to one class this term. They're canceling my class next semester. So that's another piece of income lost. And my forest service job isn't near enough to pay for all this." He waved his hand in a wide sweep, indicating the house, the barn, the Jeep, the car, the land.

He told me that they hadn't paid their mortgage in full for two months. Mom had been scrambling to find more donors but without any luck. "We're so far behind at this point. Last time we refinanced, the real estate market was booming. Now this place is worth . . . well, not as much. Not nearly as much as we owe. And even if it were, there aren't any buyers. Not even if we wanted to parcel the place up."

"Dad," I interrupted, thinking on what he'd said

yesterday, about all of us ending up on the street. "What's going to happen to us?"

He stood up and walked a little ways away from me. Picked up his binoculars like he was staring at a bird. But I knew there wasn't any bird, not at that moment, and after a bit he put the binoculars down. "I know you love this place, Wren," he said. "I used to love it too. I was born here just like you. But now I feel like it's time to let go. I know you heard what Holly said the other day, and it's true. This place was built on blood. Our family ought never to have kept it."

Panic rose in my chest. "But Dad, we *didn't* keep it," I said, scrambling. "Not really. I mean, the house is gone. And we don't grow crops. We just keep horses. Everything is different from what it used to be."

"Wren," Dad said. "It's not different enough. Ever since we found out about James, I feel like I'm living at a crime scene. An unspeakable crime scene. And I can't stand it. I don't want a single blade of grass from this place."

"But—but all that was so long ago." I was pleading now. "It shouldn't have anything to do with us anymore."

"When I was a boy, I thought that too," Dad said. "I never let myself think about the things that went on here. Even after I grew up and should've known better, I thought that it didn't have anything to do with me. Then we found out about James. And my thoughts changed, Wren. Or they didn't change so much as they got louder. So I couldn't pretend I didn't hear them anymore."

I interrupted him before he could say anything else. I didn't want to hear that horrible word, "slave." I didn't want to feel this guilt over something I'd never done. I couldn't bear it.

"Dad," I said. "I just want to know what's going to happen."

He didn't answer me right away, just started walking again. I followed him up the hill, out of the trees, near to where Tim and I had sat the day before. Dad had a big mosquito bite over his eye. I could see it starting to puff out from his skin. It made him look weirdly young, that mosquito bite. I wanted it to go away. He picked up his binoculars again and pointed them up at the sky, toward a raptor that circled above us. Then he handed the binoculars to me so I could see it was a red-tailed hawk. While I stared at the bird, Dad found the words to tell me, and it was ugly. Not the bird. But what all would happen to us. He told me as plain as he could, and all the while I listened to him I didn't move, or take my eyes off that bird.

It would take awhile for the bank to foreclose. They were so backed up it could take a year or more. Mom and Dad would use that time to adopt out all the horses and get rid of most of our stuff. He kept using the word "downsize," like we were some sort of corporation instead of a family.

"Where will we live?" I asked him, when it seemed like he was done talking.

"We'll look for an apartment."

"An apartment!" How were we going to fit into an apartment? We were *farm* people, not *apartment* people. "What about Daisy?"

"We won't go anywhere we can't take Daisy."

"Are we going somewhere we can take the barn cats?"

"We're going to find homes for them, Wren. We're going to get our house in order."

Get our house in order. It didn't make sense. *This* was our house. How could leaving it be getting it in order?

"I'm not leaving!"

"I know how you feel, Wren…"

"No," I yelled. "You actually don't." I took the binoculars off and shoved them into his hands. Then I turned and ran as fast as I could back through the woods. Dad followed me a little while, until his footsteps slowed down and then stopped altogether. But I kept running, all the way to the paved road, and since I couldn't think of anything else in the world to do, I just kept on running till the sound of my own breath drowned out every single thought in my head. I ran all the way to Tim's house.

By the time I got there I was drenched in sweat, and I knew my face was beet red. Thank goodness he was the one who opened the door.

"Wren," he said, sounding real surprised. "What's wrong?"

I couldn't think of what to say. I just saw him standing there, all sweet and worried, and I stepped forward and fell into his arms. And you know what? They felt exactly the way I'd imagined they would. They felt strong, and willing to hold me tight for as long as I needed. In that moment I felt too exhausted and too defeated even to cry. I just buried my face in Tim's chest while he rocked me back and forth.

His parents had gone out to lunch, so we had the place to ourselves. Once I got myself under control, Tim led me though the house—everything seemed sparkling clean and new—to his bathroom so I could take a shower. He gave me a flannel robe, and as I wiped the steam off the mirror with the sleeve, which was a million miles too long for me, I heard the doorbell ring. I knew it would be my parents, or at least one of them, so even though my clothes were gross and sweaty, I put them back on to prevent Dad having a heart attack. When I got downstairs, Tim was calmly saying, for what must have been the third or fourth time, that I was very upset and couldn't talk to anyone right now.

Dad, almost as tall as Tim but not quite, was working up a lather on the front porch. Probably up until this minute he'd tried to be reasonable, but now the sight of me standing back there in the living room, my hair all wet, was more than he could bear.

"Look," he shouted at Tim. "This is my daughter we're talking about. Just who the hell do you think you are?"

To me it sounded like a rhetorical question, but I guess it didn't to Tim, because he thought about it for a second. Then he said, "I'm the man she ran to, sir."

And he shut the door, firmly but gently, right in my father's face.

Seven

I wanted to call Allie and tell her about what was happening with the farm. At the same time, I couldn't stand to think of saying any of it out loud. It felt too intense to talk about over the phone. This wasn't like finding out Ry had a girlfriend—by now I had to admit that was just a pretend problem. This was all about my home, my entire life. The words "we're losing our farm" were too horrible to say. And—I know this was awful of me—but it almost made me feel ashamed, like our family had something wrong with us. It would be better to tell her at school, when I could see her face react to everything.

On Monday, Tim and I sat together on the way to school. He asked me if my parents were mad at me, or at him, and I told him that, weirdly, they didn't seem to be. At one point he said, "You should come over for a swim before it gets too cold." We both knew it wouldn't get too cold till sometime near Thanksgiving, so I said, "Yeah, that'd be fun."

When the bus pulled up at school, Allie stood waiting for me on the sidewalk. She peered through the windows and saw me sitting next to Tim. We got off the bus, and you'd never have known when she said hi that anything in the world was wrong. She waited until Tim got a few steps ahead. Then she lit into me.

"Why didn't you call me?" she asked, sounding furious.

"I did!"

"*One time.*" Like that didn't count at all.

"I'm sorry," I said. "Things were real bad at the farm this weekend."

I guess she didn't hear me, because instead of asking about the farm, she said, "I know all about Tim coming over to your house. I suppose there's a reason you didn't tell me?"

I wondered how she knew but didn't bother asking about it. Allie stood there, towering over me, looking fierce. If she'd looked at all like she had hurt feelings, I think I might have softened. But she looked purely mad, like I'd broken some strict law she'd laid down for me.

"I didn't tell you," I said, trying to keep my voice calm, "because I knew you'd be mad. Which I guess was right."

This dark look came over her face. Then she said, quiet but deadly serious, "Wren Piner. You knew that I like him. I've liked him since sixth grade. We said before school even started that if he were going to be anyone's boyfriend, he would be mine."

That was about the stupidest thing I had ever heard her say. Tim was not some front seat you could call shotgun for. At the same time it sounded sort of right, because I did feel guilty, and I found myself wishing I could just tell her the truth and clear everything up. Tim being gay wasn't a big deal. Allie didn't care about things like that any more than I did.

But I'd promised Tim. I promised him. So I shoved that thought right back out of my head. And also there was that little tiny part—another one of those horrible parts of me— that knew I could protest about Tim not being my boyfriend till the cows came home. But truthfully, that was beside the point, because I *wanted* him to be my boyfriend. No matter if he wasn't interested in me that way. No matter how much Allie liked him.

"Allie," I said, using the stern but careful voice I used with Pandora when she tried to graze with the bit in her mouth. "I didn't say anything because I didn't want you to be mad. But nothing is happening between Tim and me. I promise you. We're just friends."

She softened a little at this, but I could tell she didn't 100 percent believe me. Then she said, "Well. If that's true, did you ask him if he liked me?"

I figured she was already so mad I might as well get this

part out of the way so maybe we could all move on to a less complicated existence. "I asked him if he liked anyone in particular, and he said he didn't like any girl at Williamsport High."

That dark look came back. "Any girl but you, you mean."

"Any girl at all," I said firmly, still not able to figure out how it could be my fault if he *did* like me. Even though he *didn't*. But Allie just flounced away and avoided me the whole rest of the week, the longest we'd gone without talking in our lives. And guess what? By Friday she was dating Devon Kelly.

The next week I went to the hospital to have my hand checked out. James has privileges at Williamsport General, so every other Monday he came out to see me for a special appointment. Luckily for me, the time he had free was early in the afternoon, so I missed school instead of rehearsal.

I sat on the exam table, watching James unwrap my bandage. Mom waited outside. Ever since I ran over to Tim's, she and Dad had been strangely distant, almost like they were afraid of me and what I might do.

I wondered if anyone had told James about losing the farm. I sure couldn't bring myself to say anything. I didn't want to think about it *or* talk about it. Just saying it out loud would make everything *real*.

James cleaned my hand carefully and looked at it under lights. "How's the pain, Wren?" he said.

"It's better," I said. "I hardly even need ibuprofen any-more."

He stood there turning my hand this way and that, check-ing to see if it was healing the way it should, and while he stared at it so carefully I stared at *him* carefully, trying to figure if he was okay or still pining for Holly. James was the one person who might actually be happy to hear the farm—*the plantation*—was on its way out of our family for good. At the same time I knew he could never be glad about some-thing that would cause us so much sadness. It all just sucked.

James's face looked full of concentration. Probably there should have been some kind of awkwardness, some kind of tension between us, but it only felt like two normal people, a grown-up and a kid, a doctor and a patient. James stud-ied this injury of mine so carefully. He wished for me to be well and used his expertise to help that along. His hands felt chapped, probably because he had to wash them all the time. I tried to conjure up in my head all this history between us, the way we sort of came from the same place. But because of all the particulars, I couldn't bear to think about it for more than a minute.

James said, "That was a big sigh, Wren. Everything okay?"

"Yes, sir," I said. I hadn't even realized that I'd sighed at all. "Sorry about that."

"You don't have to be sorry."

"I just wish life didn't have to be so complicated all the time."

James smiled, but it was a sad smile. "I wish it too, Wren," he said. "I wish it too."

In place of my big bandage James gave me a package of fingerless gloves made out of gauze. I could change them myself as often as I wanted, and I could go riding again. Best of all for my mother, I could even shovel manure again. My fingertips were healed well enough that I didn't need anything covering them. Yay! I felt a lot more normal. Plus, it made it easier for me to hang on to the broom I had to dance around with during the "Necessity" song.

In the play, Caroline Jones played this girl named Susan who couldn't speak—she only danced. Watching her up there on stage, she was so graceful and perfect. One day she sat in the back row with Tyler and me and asked if she could see my burn. Even though I wasn't supposed to, I pulled off my glove. It looked a lot better than it used to—all the little blisters had flattened out by now—but even so she drew in her breath.

"I am never drinking another drop of alcohol," she said. "Never in my life. At least not until college."

Tyler snorted like he didn't believe her. I laughed. "It's not so bad," I said.

"It's the worst thing I ever did," Caroline admitted.

I racked my brain, trying to think of the worst thing that I had ever done. The first thing I came up with was dating Tim, even though we obviously weren't dating. It was just that I felt so bad about Allie and me not talking, and I made up my mind then and there to clear the air with her. I knew that if my mother hadn't been so wrapped up with the farm, that's what she would have told me to do. For the last couple of weeks, the two people I talked to the most—Allie and my mom—had been pretty much off-limits.

Because of that, the new main person I talked to was Tim. Just like Allie, everybody in the play seemed to think we were together. Caroline Jones even made a point of telling me she had no hard feelings about it, and that we made a cute couple. For some reason I found this very flattering, so much that I didn't correct her. I should have, but I didn't. That afternoon at Tim's pool, I told him about what Caroline said, and he liked it as much as I did.

"I always felt bad dating Caroline when I could never feel the same way she did," he said. We sat up to our necks in the shallow end, me with my burned hand resting on the pool deck. Nobody else was there, being as it was almost dinnertime. "But with you, you know everything, so it works out perfectly."

I could see what he meant. We never had to tell a lie, or even pretend; we just had to do what came pretty naturally, which was hang out together. So for Tim, it did work out perfectly. For me, not so much. I liked the idea of what people thought, that Tim was my boyfriend, a whole lot better than the truth. At the same time I felt bad that Tim had to walk around hiding the truth. So I said, "Maybe it doesn't always have to be such a big secret. People might surprise you. I don't think anyone would really care one way or the other."

"No," Tim said, his voice so firm he hardly sounded like himself. "They'd care. They'd see me different. I mean, you've heard Devon."

"Yes, I have heard Devon," I said. "Doesn't that bug you? It sure bugs me."

Tim waved this aside like it was nothing. "Devon's just being Devon. I think he says those things so nobody will think *he's* gay."

"Do you think Devon's gay?" This thought really surprised me.

"No," Tim said, "I don't. But since he knows it's pretty much the worst thing anyone *can* think, he makes sure and says those things. You know? Anyway, friends would be bad enough, but what would be really bad is if my parents found out."

"You think they'd mind?"

"Wren. They'd go nuts. Our church is already freaking out because of the gay ministers. So our pastor is going to split from the national branch and join this new bunch of

Lutherans who pretty much say they hate all gay people."
Tim got quiet, then added, "I don't think my father would
ever speak to me again."

"Come on," I said. "You're his *son*."

Tim looked at me like I didn't know what I was talking
about. I couldn't think of anything I could do, ever, that
would make my parents not speak to me. Even though
things at home were tense, I knew that I could rob every
bank in Williamsport and my mom would still show up at
the jail every Saturday with a stack of horse magazines and
a box of pralines.

"Here's how I figure it," Tim said. "When I go to college,
maybe then I'll meet someone. And I'll have to tell my parents, tell everyone. But until then, why rock the boat?"

I could see his point about this. "But you know," I said,
nodding my head in agreement, "one person who wouldn't
care at all would be Allie. We could tell her."

"She'd tell Devon."

"She might not tell him, if we told her not to." But even as
I spoke I wasn't absolutely sure about this, not like I would
have been even a month before.

"Still," Tim said. "I don't want to risk it. Okay? Look at
that poor kid Jesse. No way am I going to be *that* guy."

Jesse Gill hadn't made the play. Every time I saw him, he
was all by himself. I heard that guys in gym class wouldn't
let him in the showers, and I saw myself that someone wrote

a gross word on his locker. It was too bad he hadn't just stayed at Cutty River, where you could get detention just for using the word "retard". A girl I knew called *herself* a retard and got three straight days of detention. Thinking about this, I felt anger brewing. Why shouldn't Jesse be able to be at Williamsport and not get harassed?

So I could sure see why Tim would want to avoid Jesse's fate. Since pretty much everyone in the school adored Tim, he had a long way to fall. So I assured him I would keep my promise and never say a word, not to anyone. Tim still looked worried, almost like he wished he hadn't told me, so I added, "Promise!" And I vowed then and there not to ask him again if I could tell anyone. I wondered if he had any idea that Allie had a big crush on him. I felt like telling him, and might have—but that would have shown I couldn't keep a secret, which was the last message I wanted to get across.

I moved a little closer to Tim, and he draped his arm around me. It's hard to find words to tell you how good it felt, and I closed my eyes and reveled a little bit in the moment. When I opened my eyes, I saw a proper-looking blond lady in high heels open the pool gate and come click-clacking over to us. She wore lipstick and had kind of poufy, perfect hair.

"Well, hi, honey," she said to Tim. I couldn't see her eyes because they were shaded by big, dark sunglasses. I scootched a little away from Tim, and his arm slid off my shoulders.

"Hi, Mom," Tim said. "This is my friend Wren."

"Hello, Mrs. Greenlaw," I said.

Mrs. Greenlaw knelt by the pool and held her hand out to me. I reached over and shook it, even though I was dripping wet. "You're the girl who hurt her hand," she said, looking at my gauze glove. "How's it healing, honey?" She had one of those deep, melodic North Carolina accents, like she'd grown up close to the mountains.

"It's much better," I told her.

"I'm so glad. Would you like to come back to the house and have dinner with us?"

"I'd love to, ma'am, but I'm expected home. Thank you for asking me, though."

Mrs. Greenlaw stood up and smoothed out her skirt, even though it hadn't wrinkled a bit. I knew from Tim that she worked in real estate. I pictured my own mother with her baggy Levi's and dirty fingernails and tried to imagine what it would be like to live in a house with someone who looked so picture perfect.

"Honey," Mrs. Greenlaw said. Tim and I looked up at the same time, since that was what she'd been calling both of us. "Why don't you take my car and drive Wren home? It's almost time for dinner, and I'm sure you both have homework."

Mrs. Greenlaw's car smelled like perfume. It was the cleanest I'd ever seen, not a single crumb or envelope or CD case anywhere in sight. I asked Tim if it was new.

"No," he said. "She has to keep it clean because she drives clients around."

"I could never keep anything this clean," I said.

When we pulled up to my house I saw Aunt Holly's car, but the only person outside was Mom, on the front stoop, talking on the phone. I said good-bye to Tim, then went over and sat down next to her. My conversation with Tim had made me feel a little warmer toward my own mother. I could tell she was wrapping up the call, with lots of "okays" and "thank yous."

"Good news," she said to me, when she hung up. "A man up in Virginia is going to adopt Vixen and Maurice. He's going to come get them this weekend."

"What man?" I said, amazed. People didn't just pop out of the blue to adopt horses. It had always been Mom's strictest rule not to let anyone take a horse until she inspected their facility.

"Oh, a man who just bought a farm and wants a couple horses. He sounds really nice." She tried to make her voice all bright and enthusiastic, but the minute she finished talking she burst into tears.

"Oh, Mom." I put my arms around her. If it made my heart hurt—thinking how it would be these next months, watching trailers come to take our horses one by one—I couldn't imagine how it was for my mother.

From inside the house I could hear Dad and Holly

talking. Their voices sounded light and airy. I'd noticed lately that a change had come over Dad. You'd never guess he'd just lost his job and his family home. He looked like the whole weight of the world had been lifted. He had this little spring in his step, and Holly's voice sounded happier than I'd heard her in months.

"I get it," Mom said, like she'd been reading my mind. "I understand why it's a relief for them. But I just can't be happy about it. I can't be."

"It feels like the end of the world," I said, though I wish I hadn't, because Mom started in crying all over again.

Lately, in American history, Allie sat next to Devon instead of me. But on Wednesday I decided I was sick of the whole thing and plopped down right beside her. Devon wasn't there yet, and neither was Ms. Durand.

"Hey," I said to Allie, like nothing had ever happened.

"Hey," she said, like she didn't sound too sure.

"So what I want to know is," I said, "after twelve million years being best friends, are you really going to break up with me because of some boy?"

"God, Wren," Allie said. She laughed a little, but she still didn't sound invested in the conversation. As usual these days, she was dressed in a careful outfit—a little shrug over a T-shirt and flowy skirt, her hair all braided, plus eye shadow and lip gloss. "You can't break up with a girl."

"Well, that's what it feels like," I said. "It feels like you broke up with me, like you're just . . . gone." I thought about saying something about the farm, but that didn't seem quite fair. And then Devon Kelly walked in. He gave me a happy little wave hello, then sat down in the desk on the other side of her. I realized she'd been saving it for him when I saw her slip a book off it and back onto her own. Then I had a bizarre thought. It was like Allie and I had suddenly traded each other in for guys—me for Tim, her for Devon.

Ms. Durand called the class to order and announced that we would start our section on the Civil War today. There were plenty of groans, and one of them was mine. The last thing I wanted to think about these days was any topic along Civil War lines. If everything was so much better now, why make ourselves feel terrible by dredging up the past?

I thought how maybe that's what Allie was doing these days, avoiding the past by avoiding me. That made me so sad I had to put my head down on the desk. After thirty seconds or so a hand patted me softly on the back. Of course it was Allie, and it gave me the strength to pick up my head and listen to the lesson, my face fixed like nothing at all was bothering me.

Eight

At lunchtime Allie, Tim, Devon, and I headed to the park across the street from school. We walked by Jesse Gill on the way. I'd just found out that he'd signed up to be a techie for *Finian's Rainbow*, and I hoped that would help him make a couple of friends. Allie and I both said hey to him as we walked by, and then Tim did too, but Devon just ignored him.

Really only seniors were allowed to leave campus during the day, but nobody said anything to us as we walked through the parking lot. One thing I noticed was that almost everyone said hi to Tim. Back at Cutty River, there had been so few of us that there weren't real distinct groups. Sure, there were people who were more popular than others, but it wasn't like here at Williamsport High, where you were either a jock or a theater person or a loner or a freak (or some combination of the last two). Though Tim was one of the rare people who fell into both of the first two categories, or maybe because of that, he seemed to float above it all. Everybody liked him. Everybody felt like if they said hi to him, he'd say hi back.

We sat at a picnic table in the park, Allie on one side with Devon and me and Tim on the other. Now that Allie was being friendly again, I knew I should tell her about everything that had been going on at home. But no way was I saying anything in front of Devon about how my whole family was going down the tubes. I watched Allie unpack her lunch, if you could call it that: an orange, an apple, and a teensy container of yogurt that might feed a baby. "Is that all you're going to eat?" I said.

"I'm on a diet," she said, and I laughed. Allie had eaten like a horse her entire life but always looked like a reed. "No, really," she said. "I've got to keep my weight down if I'm going to photograph well." She told me she'd seen a casting call on Craigslist, for extras in a movie. "It's on Friday. I'm skipping school and going down there," she said.

"Your parents are letting you?"

"What they don't know won't hurt me," she said, almost challenging. Devon laughed. Then Allie surprised me by asking, "Do you want to come with?"

"But what will you do if you get cast?" I said, ignoring the invitation for the moment. "Won't you have to have your parents' permission?"

"I'm thinking if I get cast, then I can talk them into it. And if I talk them into that, then I can talk them into the next step, and Brindle and Stirling here I come." Brindle and Stirling was the name of the agency the modeling scout worked for, the one who'd had given Allie her card. Devon grinned and put his arm around the back of Allie's chair. You could tell he loved the idea of having a model for a girlfriend. I didn't know much about movie casting, but to me "extra" sounded like people who should blend into the background, and it was hard to imagine Allie blending in anywhere. I felt a pang—I sure hoped she wasn't setting herself up for another fall.

"Shoot, I'd love to come with you, but I can't skip school," I said, finally answering her question. "I already missed a whole week when I hurt my hand."

"I'll go with you," Devon offered. Allie smiled at him but sent a wistful little look toward Tim. Devon didn't seem to notice anything, because then he asked me if I knew what I was going to do for my history project.

"Not yet," I said. Ms. Durand had assigned us a research paper on Williamsport history. It was a full-term project, one that we were supposed to work on while we studied all the different eras. We could choose any time period we wanted as long as it was before the year we were born. I dug into my brown bag for my lunch.

"I'm going to do the Ku Klux Klan," Devon said,

sounding so happy with himself, it made me think he'd only asked what *I* was doing so he could say what *he* was doing. Like he thought this topic would just be the most cheerful thing in the world. "My father says that most of the buildings at the university are named after families that belonged to the Klan after the Civil War."

I felt a stirring of butterflies in my stomach, along with a sudden rush of gratitude that there was no Piner Hall on campus.

I did not mention this out loud. It felt so good to be back on friendly terms with Allie—like something that had gone very wrong was suddenly righted—that I didn't want to jinx it. A couple of other people showed up, football friends of Devon and a cheerleader or two, and I wondered when he'd told them we'd be hanging out at the park. We had to scrunch way down the bench to make room. This guy named Jay sat across from me. I don't know anything about football, but as soon as I saw him, the phrase "middle linebacker" popped into my head. He was very wide, but muscular, with a friendly face. Allie looked happy to be with this particular bunch.

"You know, it's funny that you and Allie were best friends," Tim said later that afternoon, as we sat together in the very last row of the auditorium during rehearsal, watching Woody and Sharon, the two characters who fall in love and live happily ever.

"What do you mean were?" I asked, though I knew exactly what he meant. "We're still best friends."

Tim ignored this and said, "You're just so different. Everything about you is different. The things you like. The way you act. The things you're interested in."

I thought about this for a minute. Nobody had ever said anything like that before. Allie and I had been best friends for so long, it was a simple fact of life. And she didn't used to seem so different from me. It was only lately, with the clothes and dating Devon. She was still the same Allie inside. Except for when she thought I got something she wanted.

Still, now that she and I were on a bit better footing, I didn't want to dwell on that. So I told Tim, "It may seem like that to you. But Allie and I like some of the same things."

"No offense, but as far as I can tell, all she cares about is guys and clothes."

Poor Allie. Really she was only interested in one guy— Tim—and all the clothes and makeup were just to impress him. She had no idea she'd gone exactly the wrong direction. Then I reminded myself that no matter what direction she'd gone, she wouldn't end up with Tim liking her the way she wanted him to. And I sure knew how that felt.

"Here's something Allie and I have in common," I said. It came to me all of a sudden. It was something I'd heard my mom say, and I had never thought much about it, but suddenly I realized it was true. "We were brought up the same way," I said.

"What does that mean?"

"Well, both of us have parents who don't think money is super important. And they think everybody should be treated the same."

"They're *liberal*," Tim said.

"I guess so," I said, but that sounded too simple.

He nodded, and then went back to watching the play. Suddenly there was a ringing sound, and the action onstage stopped. Everyone started looking around to see who the culprit was, including me, until I realized the ringing was coming from my book bag. I grabbed it and ran outside as fast as I could, but not before Ms. Winters called out, "Cell phones *off*, Wren."

"Dad," I said in a mad whisper, even though by now I was standing all the way outside on the walkway in front of the theater. "You got me in trouble! We're in the middle of rehearsal."

"It's not my fault you didn't turn off your phone." Then he told me that they would pick me up after rehearsal. We were having dinner at the Indian restaurant by Allie's new house.

"Is Holly in town?" Holly is the one who always wants Indian food. Personally it makes my nose itch.

"She is," Dad said. "She says she has a surprise for us."

I could tell from his voice he already knew what the surprise was. I hoped against hope that she would announce her wedding with James was back on. And it would be all owing to me! Well, me and Caroline Jones.

When Dad was in grad school, before my grandparents left him the farm, Mom used to teach riding lessons at a private school up north. At dinner, before Holly let us in on the big surprise, she and Dad told Mom this idea they had about how she could do the same thing after the farm was foreclosed and all our horses had been given away to undeserving owners.

"There are no schools with riding programs around here," Mom said. Usually she scarfed down Indian food, but tonight she just sat there, picking up her fork and then putting it down again without eating. They had ordered a ton of rice and Indian bread and all these spicy, saucy dishes that I wouldn't touch. Instead I ordered the plainest thing on the menu, tandoori chicken.

"Who says we have to stay around here?" Dad said. "There's nothing holding us anymore. If you got a job at a boarding school, that would take care of a place to live until we got our credit back together."

"Um, hello?" I said. "To answer your question, I say we have to stay around here."

Holly and Dad looked at each other. I hated the air they

had these days, like they were so happy it didn't matter how Mom and I felt. Suddenly I didn't feel like hearing Holly's announcement about how she and James were getting back together. Like it would be this big surprise anyway, when I could see plain as day she had on her diamond ring again. I pushed my plate away. It was mostly empty anyway; unlike Mom, I can eat no matter what's happening.

"I'd like to be excused," I said.

"Excused?" Dad said. "What are you talking about, excused? We're in a restaurant."

"I can go over to Allie's." She lived just two blocks away.

"But Holly hasn't even—"

"Right, the big news. Congratulations, Holly, I'm real happy for you and James. Now I'm going, if that's quite all right with everyone." I stood up and threw my napkin on the table.

Dad opened his mouth, obviously about to say it was not one bit all right. But without even looking up, Mom said, "Just let her go, Joe. Let her go." Then she said, "Not long, honey. We'll come get you on our way home."

I wanted to say good-bye to her, but that would seem like I was saying good-bye to Dad and Holly, too. And I didn't want to say anything to them. Yes, I felt plenty glad Holly's heart wasn't broken anymore. I just wished Mom's and my hearts didn't have to break so hers could get fixed.

*   *   *

I walked past the elementary school where Allie might've gone if she hadn't started out living in Leeville. I tried to think what my life would have been like if Allie's parents had always lived in town. Maybe I would just have met her when I came to Williamsport High, and we wouldn't even have known to be friends. She would have just been some tall, fancy girl in my American history class. I never would have known about the Allie who didn't bother washing her hair or mind wearing ripped T-shirts. Then I remembered that without Allie, I probably wouldn't have gone to Williamsport High at all. I would have just stayed at Cutty River. But then I never would have gotten to sing the "Necessity" song in *Finian's Rainbow*, which had pretty much been the highlight of my life so far, even before the actual performance. And I never would have met Tim.

I wished I were walking over to his house instead of Allie's. With him I wouldn't have to explain nearly as much, plus he'd never been mad at me about anything. All of a sudden I realized that lately Tim had become my best friend instead of Allie. It felt weird how obvious this thought was, not surprising in any way. It was just how things had turned out.

By now I'd come to Allie's street. It was a nice street, with big old houses and oak trees. But it didn't have anywhere near the wild, tangled, Spanish moss feeling that my part of Leeville had. Except for the heat it could have been any-where in the world, whereas when you walked up to my house you just knew you were in the South. I tried to imag-ine moving from there to here. I did not try to imagine mov-ing up north. That possibility I could not consider for even a second.

I turned on the street before Allie's house so I could go through the alleyway and into her backyard. I thought I might find her sitting on her back stoop, watching her sister play on the swings. And in fact, that's exactly where I did find her, though unfortunately, who should be sitting right beside her but Devon.

I know it's ridiculous. But I felt this flash of jealousy. Not that I wanted Devon for a boyfriend—no way—but that maybe he had become Allie's best friend instead of me. Of course this wasn't fair at all, given as how I'd just been thinking the same thing of Tim. But in my experience jeal-ousy doesn't generally care about fair, it just rears up its ugly head and makes you feel sick right between your heart and your stomach.

"Wren!" Sylvie yelled. She jumped off her swing and ran over to give me a hug. I hugged her back, and Allie waved to me from the stoop.

"Hey, Wren," she said. "What are you doing here?"

"My parents are having dinner at the Indian restaurant," I said. I didn't say anything about Holly, because I didn't want to have to fill Devon in. "I finished early, so I thought I'd come over and say hi."

Allie and Devon took up the whole stoop, so I couldn't sit down with them. I just stood there like an idiot, grateful that hugging Sylvie gave me something to do.

"Anyway," Devon said, like he was changing the subject, even though we hadn't really been talking about anything yet. "I'd better get going." He kissed Allie and then stood up. "I'll see you, Wren," he said.

"Bye."

He walked around to the gate and left without bothering to say good-bye to Sylvie, who trotted on into the house, almost like she'd been chaperoning and now her job was done.

When I turned back to Allie, she was watching him go too. Her eyes were kind of narrow, and her forehead was all scrunched up. The gate clanged shut behind him, but she didn't say anything until we heard his car engine start.

"Did you see that?" she said. "He didn't even say good-bye to Sylvie."

I admitted I'd noticed that too.

"My mother says you can always tell the quality of a man by how he treats little children," Allie said. I could believe this, because Mrs. Hackett was always coming out with pronouncements like that. Once she'd told us in all seriousness that we should never date men who don't like cats, because it means they don't like what they can't manipulate and control. I was just about to remind Allie of this when she took me by surprise by bursting into tears.

"I hate him," she said. "Sometimes I think I really hate him." And she buried her face in her hands.

I stood staring at her—I knew I had to say *something*. All I could come up with was, "He's not so bad."

"He is," Allie said. "He *is*. He acts all nice and then he says just hateful things, and he expects me to laugh about them. And you know what else? I hate him because he's not Tim. Tim never says the kind of things Devon does."

This sense of helplessness and exasperation came over me at the same time. And I couldn't help saying, "Allie, you barely even know Tim."

"Oh, right," she spat. "Not like you do?"

I tried to steer the conversation back a little bit. "But Allie," I said. "Why are you going out with Devon, if you don't even like him?" I sat down in the spot where Devon had just been. Allie didn't answer. She just kept on crying. So I put my hand on her shoulder and went ahead and said the next logical thing. "Why don't you just break up with him? If you hate him so much?"

As abruptly as she'd started, she stopped crying. She lifted up her head, wiped her nose on her bare arm, and said, "Well, what am I supposed to do then? Who am I supposed to hang out with? You and *your* boyfriend, like I'm some third wheel?"

I took my hand off her shoulder. She would not let the conversation get steered around. And my telling her he was *not* my boyfriend for the zillionth time wasn't going to make a difference.

"I don't know," I finally said. "Maybe you should find an interest or something."

"I *had* interests," she yelled at me. "I had interest in cheer-leading and they wouldn't let me on the squad. And I had interest in modeling"—by now she had started yelling, so her mother, banging around in the kitchen on the other side of the screen door, would be sure to hear—"but I can't do that, either. So don't sit there with your perfect boyfriend and your perfect part in the play and your perfect life and tell me to find an interest."

She stood up and slammed into the house. I heard her mother say, "Allie," and then pause for a minute, like she wasn't sure if she should come outside and apologize to me, or chase Allie. Then her footsteps clomped off in the opposite direction, after her own kid.

The light outside had turned kind of flat. Any minute my parents would honk their horn in front of the house. My throat filled up with tears. It was my stupid fault Allie thought my life was so perfect, because I hadn't bothered telling her any of my problems. Now she felt bad, and I felt bad, and she was in the house crying while I sat out here very close to the same.

I stood up and walked around to the front of the house. Our station wagon came rattling up the street. Holly and Dad sat in front, looking cheerful, which made me feel even worse for my mother. Not to mention Allie, and me.

Nine

It occurs to me that I haven't said what Finian's Rainbow is all about. In case you're wondering, this Irishman named Finian moves to a pretend Southern state called Missitucky. If the people who wrote this play had decided to call the state North Caroltucky or Mississolina, you could be sure our high school would not be performing it. As things stood, it hit close enough to home to strike me as kind of a risky choice, even if it was written fifty years ago or more.

Anyway, what happens in the play is, Finian steals a pot of gold that can make wishes come true, and this leprechaun Og chases him all the way from Ireland to get it back. At one point the main girl in the play (Sharon, played by Liza Jane Rawls, a senior who hadn't spoken to me a single time) makes a wish, and then this bigoted white senator who's been mean to everyone turns into an African-American man. My mom told me that when her school did it, they just changed the kid with makeup, but as I believe I have already mentioned, in our production Tyler Caldwell played the African-American version of the senator—no makeup required.

Since Tim had a much bigger part in the play, Tyler and I would watch when he was onstage. Tyler told me how he hoped his ACL would heal in time for him to play baseball in the spring.

"I hope Tim doesn't blow off baseball," Tyler said. "He's really good."

"He's good at this, too," I whispered, kind of wishing Tyler would stop talking. I just wanted to listen to Tim. He was singing this funny song called "Something Sort of Grandish," with all these nonsense words. Tim made it sound so hilarious and charming, I thought that the only problem with the play would be nobody'd believe Sharon liked Woody better than Og.

Tyler nodded. "It would be cool if he could do both things," he whispered. But of course there was no way Tim could do two activities that took up so much time, and Ms. Winter had said something about doing a Shakespeare play in the spring, which wouldn't be as much fun as a musical. Maybe Tim would play baseball instead. I thought about what a good athlete he was, and how that was just one of the reasons nobody would ever guess he was gay—yeah, a total stereotype. But now he had chosen theater instead. I knew all about stereotypes and how they were stupid, but I had to admit I worried that Tim was kind of conforming to the stereotype by giving up sports for theater, not to mention playing a leprechaun. A *singing* leprechaun, who would probably be wearing green tights. I just didn't want to see him get in a situation he didn't want to be in yet. Sometimes I'd sneak little looks at Tyler, wondering if he could guess about Tim, and I realized part of the reason he couldn't might be that he thought Tim was going out with me. It made me feel kind of important, protecting Tim, and almost made up for the fact that he could never be what I wanted.

Still I wondered about the musical theater piece of the puzzle, and later on I went ahead and asked Tim about it. I didn't worry that he would get offended. Lately he and I had been talking about everything. I think it was kind of a relief for him being able to say this stuff out loud.

As usual, we were taking the late bus home to Leeville, sitting all the way in the back. I asked him if he thought his secret was safer when he played football. "It's a stupid stereotype," I said, "but doesn't that mean stupid people get that idea in their heads?"

"Here's the thing," Tim said. "Ever since I was little, I loved playing ball. Football, baseball, all of it. I used to sleep with my dad's old college football. But you know, I also thought it'd be fun to be in a play. Everyone's told me forever that my voice isn't half-bad. Plus, I wanted to get out of the locker room for a while."

I wondered if it was because everyone showers together, but saying this out loud seemed like going too far, so I just said, "Why?"

"Because of all the trash talking. You wouldn't believe the stuff guys say."

"I've heard plenty of trash talk," I assured him.

"Well, it's way worse when it's just guys. And in the locker room, it's faggot this and fairy that. This kid Devereaux was on the baseball team for like a week freshman year, and word got out he was gay, and everybody just tortured him. They wouldn't let him in the showers. I thought he'd get hurt, I really did."

"I know Devereaux," I said. "He transferred to Cutty River."

"I don't have a clue if he's gay or not," Tim went on. "Just someone decided he was and that was pretty much the end. Something about him set off the alarms. You know what I mean? Like that kid Jesse. I keep thinking, if any of those guys knew about me, and then realized we were standing around getting dressed together, well, they'd just kill me. I would picture it in my head, all those fists . . . and . . . plus my friends looking so disgusted. And in theater . . . I don't have to think about it. In fact, I never think about it. And it's really great to *not* think about it, you know?"

I nodded. "It sucks you have to go through that, Tim."

He leaned his head back against the window and closed

his eyes. "Ever see a TV show called *Friday Night Lights*?" he said.

"I've heard of it," I said. I didn't tell him I had absolutely no interest in football. He must've already noticed I hadn't been to a single game.

"Well, there was this one episode where the coach's daughter happens to see the assistant coach in a gay bar. So a day or two later she goes up to him and tells him not to worry, she won't tell anyone. And he says to her, his face totally blank, 'Tell anyone what?' Like it's just too terrible a thing, in the football world, to even mention the word. I kept watching that show, waiting for them to bring up that story line again. But they never did. That was that. You're gay, it's football, it's the South. Keep it to yourself."

"Well," I said. "That was on TV. I mean, in real life, there might be a jerk or two. But most of your friends, I mean your real friends, might not even care."

The bus wheezed and whistled to a stop at the end of my driveway, and the driver flicked out the little stop sign.

"They'd care," Tim said, instead of good-bye, as I stood to leave. "Believe me, they'd care."

When I got to the house, my mom's car and trailer were gone. Dad sat at the picnic table, looking over his lesson plan for the next day.

"Where'd Mom go?" I asked, petting Daisy.

Dad put his pen down and took off his glasses. This was a new gesture he had, new not only since he started wearing those glasses but since the farm started really and truly slipping away. Before he gave news that might cause some kind of reaction, he would take his glasses off and stare a minute, maybe to let his eyes adjust.

"She took Brutus over to Knockton Farms," he said. "They're going to use him for lessons."

I stopped short, not believing what I'd just heard. Lessons!

"But—but—he's *retired*," I stuttered. "Brutus . . . the poor guy worked hard his whole life, and now he's *retired*. You can't just send him back to work. Mom said she'd never give any horse to Knockton." Brutus had been with us almost as long as Pandora—and the awful thought struck me: One of these days I would come home to find Pandora, the only thing I'd ever want to take with me to a desert island, sold to some summer camp or riding school. Sold to some Wilbur Beach ten-year-old who'd taken a passing fancy to horses.

My dad started to say something, but I didn't want to hear it. "I'm going for a ride," I said, and stalked off toward the stables. Daisy started to follow me, but Dad called her back. I saddled up Pandora and took off down the road. I galloped past Cutty River Landing, past the turnoff for the Old Farthing Road, over through Allie's old neighborhood. I rode till dusk, till the night started cooling off. What I really wanted to do was ride Pandora someplace where no one could ever take her away. But once the sun went down I began shivering in my short sleeves, so I headed home, realizing with a sob in my throat that there wasn't any such place anymore. Not really.

Back at the barn I already had Pandora out of her tack and was brushing her down before I heard my mom. She was crying again—the sound so muffled and soft, I had to stop brushing to make sure I knew what I was hearing.

Sure enough I found her sitting in Brutus's empty stall, crying. I tiptoed across the hay to sit down next to her.

She lifted her face and wiped her nose on her shirt. "I hoped you wouldn't hear me," she said.

"I heard you."

"I mucked out the straw and spread fresh hay," Mom said. "Then I realized—I'm an idiot!—I realized there wasn't any need to spread fresh hay because Brutus isn't coming back. And then I realized there may never be another horse in this stall again. By this time next year this whole barn might be torn down."

That was too much for me. My thought had been to comfort my mother, but when she said that, *I* burst out crying. Mom leaned into me and said, "I'm sorry, Wren. I'm truly sorry."

We sat there for a long time. I tried to focus on the smell of a freshly mucked stall with its good clean straw, and the snorts and breathing of the horses that we still had left. Sweet manure and fresh straw, the breath and shuffling of our horses.

When I told Tim about Brutus, he didn't say much, just listened and nodded like he understood, and put his arm around me. I made a little note in my head about how this can be the absolute best thing to do for a person who's feeling down. Usually what I want to do is blab on about all the ways everything will turn out okay. But if anyone had told me it would turn out okay, I might have been tempted to punch him right in the nose.

The other night, after Allie yelled at me over at her house, I'd sent her a text saying I was sorry that I'd upset her. She didn't answer, and all week we'd been avoiding each other. When she wasn't in American history on Friday, I remembered that she was skipping school to try out for that movie. Devon sat on the other side of her empty desk, in his usual spot. I guess he'd decided not to go with her after all.

"Hey," I said to him.

"Hey," he said back. I leaned over to pull my books out of my bag, and when I sat up I saw he'd plopped a piece of paper in front of me.

"What's this?" I said, picking it up.

"It's the list," he said, "of local families who used to belong to the Klan."

My heart did a somersault, I swear. I slid my hands into my lap to keep from snatching at the paper and tried to look as though I didn't care as my eyes scanned the list. I could hardly read, I was so scared that I'd see the name Piner.

But guess what? Our name wasn't there! I tried not to let out a huge sigh of relief. There were plenty of names I *did* recognize. This could make me a bad person, but for a moment that made me feel better. For example, I saw the name Kendall on the list, and there sat Hilary Kendall right in the front row, chatting with the person next to her like she didn't have a care in the world. And her family had been in the Klan! The Klan had done a lot of damage here after the Civil War, I knew that already. They had burned down the offices for the African-American newspaper and run a lot of newly prosperous African Americans out of town. But was Hilary Kendall brooding over this? No, she was not. She was just laughing and waiting for Ms. Durand to show up like the rest of us.

I passed the list back to Devon. He smiled like he never would've guessed his project could worry me. Of course, since his family came from up north, he probably just didn't get it.

"I wonder how it's going for Allie at the tryouts," I said, not wanting him to know I felt relieved not to see my name on the list.

"She just texted me," Devon said. "She's still waiting, but she made the first cut."

Huh. Allie texted Devon while still giving me the silent treatment? That didn't feel too good. So I focused back to the discovery about my family at least not being so bad as I thought. Maybe we hadn't been helping out the Underground Railroad or anything, but maybe after the war our heads had got turned around. Good people like Dad and Holly didn't just come out of nowhere, right? Maybe I had relatives who fought against the Ku Klux Klan, or helped out with that newspaper. Maybe I would even research *that* for my American history project!

After class, I ran into Tim by his locker. He was talking to that football player, Jay, who kind of waved at me instead of saying hi, and I tried to remember if I'd heard him say a single word yet.

"Hey, Wren," Tim said. He gave me this friendly little chuck under my chin. It may have been my imagination, but I thought I saw the girl at the next locker looking over like she wished Tim would be flirty like that with her. The three of us started walking down the hall together. Tim told me about a party that Saturday night over at one of the cheerleaders' houses. Given everything that was going on at home—not to mention what had happened to me at my last party—I didn't feel too optimistic about being allowed to go. I wasn't even sure I'd have the heart to ask, but who knew, maybe I'd get brave.

*   *   *

I have to say, the thought of digging up my family's secret honorable past cheered me up considerably. That afternoon when I got home from rehearsal, I saw the farrier's truck parked out by the barn, and I went right on out there to help. She and my mom had one of the newer horses out. He looked pretty skittish—none of us had ridden him yet—and even though they had tied him pretty good, he kept slamming one row of the stalls and then the other. "Hey, Trudy," I said to the farrier. She looked up, and the horse pulled his hoof right out of her hand.

"Sorry about that," I said.

"It's okay," Mom said. "Could you hold his head, see if you can keep him calm?"

I walked around and grabbed onto his halter. Mom had named him Ulysses when he first came, early last summer, but for some reason we'd been calling him Rex. He was an especially beautiful horse—black, with only the tiniest white dot between his eyes. I lifted my gauzy hand and placed it over the dot, whispering at him to hush and stand still. "They only want to fix your feet," I told him. Rex had sand cracks when he first came to stay, something horses get from training too much on hard surfaces. My breath made his ears twitch a little, but he seemed to quiet down; he let me scratch him under the chin, and Trudy and Mom got a good look at all his hooves.

"They're much better," Trudy told Mom. She dropped his hoof and stood up straight. "Just keep up with the moisturizer, and he should still be taking it easy."

Mom nodded, then said to me, "Wren, can you take him back out to the pasture?"

She and Trudy went into the little office. Trudy worked pretty cheap for my mom, giving her a rescue discount, but I had a feeling Mom was going to tell her they wouldn't be paying her at all. So when I peered into the office as I unclipped Rex, it surprised me to see Mom writing a check from her ledger.

By the time I got back to the barn, Trudy had packed up and left. I asked Mom about the money. "Oh, Wren," she said. "I don't want you worrying about all that."

"Mom," I said. I knew my voice sounded stern, but I didn't care. "How could I not worry about it? Just how do you think that would that be possible?"

She sighed and pushed the hair out of her face. Then she put her elbow through mine, and we walked out of the barn. "You're right, Wren. Of course this affects you just as much as us. I just wish it didn't. I wish things were different."

"But they're not different," I said, "and it just makes me feel worse when you don't tell me what's going on."

Mom looked at me the way she does sometimes, when she remembers that I'm sixteen instead of six. I saw her take a deep breath. "Okay," she said. "You know how Dad told you we stopped paying the mortgage? Well, that's freeing up a little cash for the moment while Dad's still getting paid, plus there were donations for the horses that got adopted. I can pay for some necessities, but we do need to try to hang on to what money we've got before we decide what our next move will be."

"But you don't know what that is," I said, exasperated.

"No," Mom admitted. "It could take a long time for the bank to get around to getting rid of us. Not that I want this to drag on forever. Believe me."

"I hate that Dad's happy about it." There, I'd said it. We were about halfway to the house at this point. The fact that I hadn't seen any sign of Daisy made me think Dad had probably gone on one of his bird walks.

"Oh, honey," Mom said. "He's not happy. He grew up here. He loves it just as much as you do."

I stopped walking and glared at her, hoping my dark expression would remind her she'd agreed to level with me. She took another deep breath.

"I think for Dad," she said, "it's like facing the music. Finally the worst is happening, but at least he doesn't have to *worry* about the worst happening. Because it's already come. And you know, the past has always weighed heavily on him. It did on his father, too."

"Sooo—they wanted to get away from the past," I said. "But they couldn't bear to get rid of this place."

"And now this place is getting rid of itself," Mom said. She said it with a catch in her voice. We stood on a little rise, so we could see beyond the east pasture, the rows of brick houses that made up Cutty River Landing. All those houses were built on what used to be cotton fields.

Mom followed the direction of my gaze. "There are a lot of ghosts," she said, "and there's a lot of shame. A whole lot of shame. You can't blame Dad if a part of him feels glad to leave that behind him."

She reached out and took my right hand—the good, ungloved one. Part of me wanted to tug away from her. But I didn't. I just started walking again, and so did she, the two of us hand in hand toward the house that was still ours, at least for a little while longer.

Ten

Speaking of holding hands, on Monday morning as I collected my books from my locker, I saw Devon walking down the hall, holding hands with a small, dark-haired girl I didn't know. I did know she was a freshman, though, because Allie had pointed her out as one of the few who'd made the cheerleading squad. *Hello?* I thought. Hadn't Allie been his girlfriend just this past Friday? She'd texted him about the auditions, after all. What the heck had happened since then? I wondered if Devon had been with this girl at the party on Saturday, which I never did get around to asking if I could attend. I knew Tim went because on Sunday he and I went swimming at his pool. His head was hurting real bad and his eyes were all bloodshot. He hadn't said a single thing about Devon and Allie. Except for complaining about his hangover, the only thing he told me about the party was that Jay drove him home. I wondered what it was like to sit in a car with someone who never said a word.

When I got to American history, Allie was sitting way in the back. Devon sat right up front, his long legs stretched out under the desk, not caring who he might trip. He smiled at me as I walked by, like he thought I wouldn't even care about what he'd done to Allie. I didn't smile back, but I did say, "Hey, Devon," like nothing he'd ever done could possibly bother me or anybody else. Then I headed straight toward the seat next to Allie.

Allie didn't look up as I slid into the desk next to her. She was wearing this floppy blue hat with a yellow flower on it, and the brim kind of hid her face. I ripped out a sheet of paper from my notebook.

What happened? I wrote, thinking it might be easier for her to write and answer than say anything out loud.

Broke up with me, she wrote back, in the saddest little letters you ever saw. At this point Ms. Durand came in, so I couldn't say anything. I just looked at her in a way that I hoped told her I was sorry she felt so bad.

After class Allie and I headed outside to the little stone wall that overlooked the football field. Hardly anyone was out there this time of day, so we could have some privacy. I'd be late for English, but talking to Allie was more important. She took off her hat and put it on the wall next to her, and then she pulled a little brush out of her bag and started attacking her hair with these hard, furious little strokes. I could hear the strands popping and crackling.

"I don't know what's wrong with me," she said, as she brushed. "I didn't even like him."

"You *hated* him," I said, giving the word extra dramatic emphasis so that even she had to laugh. "Maybe that's why he did it," I went on. "Who wants to go out with someone who hates you?"

"No," she said. "That's not why. He hooked up with that girl Rachel on Saturday. My parents wouldn't let me go to the party, of course. I don't know why they don't rename me Rapunzel and lock me up in a tower." Allie whacked her brush against the wall, then told me what happened at the film try-outs. She hadn't gotten a part as an extra, but one of the casting directors offered to get her an appointment with a local model-ing agent. So when she got home she confessed to her parents, hoping they might change their minds about her modeling. But instead they grounded her for the next two weeks.

"Two *weeks*! They just don't get it," Allie said. "Nothing ever works out for me anymore, and the one thing I possibly *could* do, they won't *let* me do."

Poor Allie. I racked my brain for something cheerful I could say, but honestly everything did seem awfully bleak.

Allie said, "I wish I'd never even come to this school. Maybe we should just go back to Cutty River."

I froze. I didn't want to go back to Cutty River School, not one single bit. So far things *were* working out for me here. And I'd come here in the first place because Allie'd wanted me to. I wasn't going to leave now just because she hadn't made the cheerleading squad or landed the boyfriend of her choice. I felt bad for her, I really did. Last spring, Allie and I'd been a kind of team. A two-for-one deal. Now I felt more like just one person, and I was finding out I liked it that way.

But of course I couldn't come right out and say this. And I thought, *Maybe now's the time to come clean and tell her about the farm.* "The truth is," I said, "I don't know where I'll go to school next year. Because my parents are losing the farm."

"What do you mean, losing the farm?"

Hearing Allie say this, her face all confused like it couldn't possibly be true, made me feel very shaky. So I said the rest real fast. "I mean, my parents can't pay their mortgage anymore. They're going to get foreclosed on, and we have to move."

"That's terrible," Allie said. But she sounded kind of matter-of-fact, not like she really meant it. She picked up her floppy hat and pulled it down almost to her eyes.

"Yeah," I agreed. "And the one thing we know is, we can't stay there forever." That last phrase made my whole throat seize up. Allie reached out and put her hand over mine, the left one, which still had its gauzy glove. I could feel the weight and warmth from her hand but not her skin.

"Wren," she said. "It was hard for me to leave our house in Leeville. But now that we're in Williamsport, I like it just as much. I may like it even better. The town, I mean, not the school. I know it's scary to move, but you'll see. It'll be all right."

I blinked hard a couple of times, then studied her face to see if she was serious. In Leeville, Allie had lived in a nice house out on Honeysuckle Drive. It'd had a good-sized backyard with a privacy fence. The house she'd moved to in Williamsport was almost exactly the same, except a whole lot closer to the university. Did she really think swapping one house for another would be the same as losing the land where your whole family had lived for generations? Leaving acres of live oak and Spanish moss and a rolling river, not to mention fifteen horses and four cats? Swap our nice old farmhouse for an apartment?

"Oh, sure," I said. "Probably we can bring all the horses and cats and so forth to whatever crappy little apartment we end up renting."

"The horses," Allie said, like she hadn't bothered to remember about them. "Will the person who buys your place get them?"

"No," I said, "because nobody's going to buy the place. That's what foreclosure means. The bank gets it, and I don't think a whole lot of banks care anything about rescued horses. Banks just auction everything off. And do you remember what happens to retired race horses who go to auction? The whole point of my mom rescuing them in the first place?"

I felt my eyes fill up with tears, but at that moment they were angry tears more than sad ones. Allie had been around my family and our horses so long, it seemed like she should know why my mother saved them. But she just sat there, looking disappointed that she couldn't put some sort of cheerful spin on it.

"Look," I said, pulling my hand out from under hers. My gauzy glove scraped in a way that made my palm hurt for the first time in weeks. "I'm late for English, so I'd better get going."

"Okay," Allie said. "Will you meet me for lunch, though?" She looked up at me from under the brim of that hat. And I felt sorry for her, I did. But I also felt betrayed. How could she of all people not get how bad it was to have to move away from our farm? She had practically grown up there herself! But it seemed like she thought breaking up with Devon was a worse problem. So I said, "I can't. I have work to do in the library."

Three minutes later, when I walked into English class, they were already discussing a Langston Hughes poem that starts out "What happens to a dream deferred?" I just sat there thinking on how my mom's dream was saving horses, and nobody seemed to care that it was not only being deferred, it was dying.

Since I told Allie I had to go to the library instead of lunch, I figured I'd better do it. I had to start researching my paper anyway. I sat down at a computer in the far corner and went to the Google screen. Then I just sat there. I had no idea how to go about researching my own family. I thought about typing in Piner Plantation, Leeville, North Carolina, and put my fingers on the keyboard to do it. Part of me thought nothing at all would come up except my mom's horse rescue. The other part of me felt terrified about what *else* might come up. After all, when James's sister found out the information that busted him and Holly apart, the whole thing had started with an Internet search.

I sat there, fingers unmoving on the keyboard. The cursor blinked on the search bar for probably five whole minutes until a familiar voice said, "Wren. What're you doing? Aren't you hungry?"

There stood Tim, right next to me. Tim with his nice, freckly, smiley face. And this feeling I got lately came flooding over me, like the simple sight of him just made everything okay.

"Hey," I said. "I wanted to do some research on my family

in Leeville. What we were like after the Civil War. But I don't know what to search."

"Did you Google it?"

Part of me wanted to say yes I had, but nothing had come up. But I didn't want to lie to Tim. So I said, "No. I was too scared."

He nodded. I knew he'd understand. "Well, why don't you ask your dad about it?" he said. "He probably knows the history." Tim sat down in a swivel chair and pulled it close to me. "Can I show you something?"

Tim went to his e-mail and opened a note from his church. It was a mass mailing about the thing he'd mentioned before, how they were going to separate from the main Lutheran church. He clicked on a link that went to a website that was all about how bad homosexuals were. The website said some vicious things.

"There's a big meeting in Stony Mountain this weekend," Tim said. "A bunch of Lutheran pastors and church members are going to talk about forming their own separate church. One that doesn't let in faggots."

I hated hearing Tim use that word. "Is that what they said? I mean, that's how they put it?"

"No. But they might as well. They say a lot worse than that."

Tim and I sat quiet, staring at the screen. I don't know if he was reading along with me about hell, and sin, and commandments. But as I read all these things, these mean and awful things, I couldn't stand thinking of him reading them too, so I reached over his hands and x-ed out of there.

"I hate that website," I said.

"My parents are going," he said. "To the meeting. I said I couldn't go because we had rehearsals, so they're leaving me behind."

We never had weekend rehearsal, but I didn't say anything about that. After a minute Tim said, in this very calm, very empty voice, "Sometimes I think I'd rather be dead."

When I heard Tim say this, the word "dead," a feeling came over me that was cold and hot at the same time. Icy on my spine but burning in my chest. I sure hoped he was saying this as an expression, and not meaning that he would ever truly want to *die*. Because he had to know—he had to—that one day he'd be out of high school and move away from Williamsport. And then the life he *chose* could begin. And meanwhile, he had me. Even though it was hard sometimes, I sure would pretend to be his girlfriend as long as he needed me to. If it kept him safe.

"Rather be dead than what?" I said, trying to keep my voice light. "A Lutheran?"

He laughed a little, but I could see his heart wasn't in it. Then he said it again and finished the thought. "I'd rather be dead than like this, a faggot."

When he said it like that, along with that *word*, it didn't sound like an expression at all. It sounded like he meant it.

He looked like he meant it too, his face suddenly stone still, all the smiliness gone from it. I couldn't stand seeing him this way, or thinking about him hurting so bad he'd want to die.

"Tim," I said. "Can't you see it's not you that's been born a particular way? A way that's bad, I mean. You're just fine. It's all of them who are the problem. They're being hateful and mean. They're *choosing* to be hateful and mean. It's like the Klan after the Civil War. One day all these people"—I tapped the computer screen, though the site was gone— "will be ashamed of this. Or else their children will be, or their grandchildren."

I waited for Tim to nod, but he didn't. He just kept staring at the computer like that website was still there. "My parents would wish I was dead," he said. "If they ever found out."

"They wouldn't ever wish that!"

"You should hear them," he said. "My dad, he's so angry about this church thing—I never realized how much he hates homosexuals. And that means he hates me, too. He just doesn't know it yet."

I reached out and touched Tim's face. He smiled a bit but still looked so sad. My insides did this little tumble. Part of me felt like if I could only make him love me the way I loved him, all his problems would be solved. In some way I couldn't name, this thought seemed disloyal—disloyal to who Tim *was*. But as he leaned his lovely face against my hand, no other word existed for how I felt. I loved him. I just did. I couldn't help it.

Once, ages ago, my mother and I rode up on an elevator with two men who were holding hands. It couldn't have been in Williamsport—we don't have many elevators, let alone men who hold hands in public. So we must have been traveling somewhere, maybe in Boston visiting her parents. I guess I'd have been about five years old, maybe six, and I'm sure no one had ever told me anything about homosexuals. Certainly nobody had ever told me being gay was bad or wrong. At the same time I knew what I saw was not usual—two men holding hands—and I kept looking over at my mother to see how she'd react. She just smiled at me, and smiled at them, and when they got off the elevator, she said, "Love is love, Wren. We smile when we see it."

Sitting there in the library, I told Tim this story. I thought it would make him happy, but it didn't. He just looked grim and said, "Well, it's too bad you're not gay instead of me."

Tim's dark mood hadn't left him by the time we rode home on the late bus after rehearsal. We didn't talk much, but I could tell he didn't want to hang out, so I just said good-bye with a little pang of loss and got off at my stop. When I got to the house, I saw Dad hosing off the ride-on mower.

I threw my backpack down on the picnic table next to Dad's old Winchester. He must've been out target practicing. Mom would give him hell if she saw it there.

"Hi, Dad," I said.

"Hi yourself." He looked surprised but happy at my sudden friendliness.

"Dad," I said. I spoke loudly over the sound of spraying water. "I want to ask you some questions about the Piner family. It's for a paper in my American history class."

Dad looked at me with this very strange expression. For a change he didn't have his glasses on, and his face seemed weirdly exposed without them. He put down the hose and went over to shut off the water. The water ran onto the ground and started soaking my sneakers, so I sat down on the bench and pulled my feet up.

"Now what's this?" Dad asked, when he came back. He sat on the other side of the table.

"Well," I said. "This boy from Wilbur Beach is writing a paper for American history about local families who belonged to the Klan."

Dad nodded, but he had a tense look on his face. I waited for him to bang his fist on the table and say, "No Piner in the history of North Carolina has ever belonged to the Klan!" But he didn't. He just sat there with an expression that seemed very un-Dad-like. A vein I didn't even know he had popped out on his forehead.

"Well," I said, feeling less confident, "I was wondering what the Piner family was like before the Civil War. For instance, maybe we set our slaves free. Or maybe after the war we helped out ex-slaves, gave them jobs and such. I thought I would find out, you know, research it, and write my paper about how maybe we weren't so bad."

Dad leaned across the table. He tapped his fingers on the board that lay exactly between him and me. "Wren," he said, in this low, growly voice, "I want to tell you something. And I'm only going to tell it to you once. I have been remiss if I have never said this to you before."

"Okay," I said, not at all wanting to hear what he had to say.

"The Piners," my father said, spitting out our last name like we were Hitler. "Your family. My family. Our ancestors. They owned slaves. Human beings. That's how they built their fortune. That's how they built this place, the ground where this picnic table is standing. Where we're sitting right now. There are no heroes in that past. There is no way to be *kind* to slaves, because there is no way to own human beings *kindly*. It is a crime against humanity. It is one of the *most serious* crimes against humanity. Do you understand that, Wren?"

"Of course I do," I said.

"I know you love this place," he said. "I love it too. But it's time to face the fact that every single acre is soaked in blood. Human blood. We should have let it go a hundred and fifty years ago. So you know what I say now? I say good riddance. I'm sorry about your mother's horses, I truly am. But to the grass they graze on, I say good riddance, and I say good-bye."

Dad stood up and started heading into the house. About halfway to the door he stopped and turned toward me. "I'm not a man who believes in censorship," he said. "But you're not to write that paper, Wren. Do you understand me? You're not to go looking for honor in our past. Because there is none. I'm sorry to be the one to tell you that. And I'm sorry I haven't made it clear before now."

Burst. Deflated. I couldn't even answer. Like I knew that eventually everyone would succeed in making me hate the place I'd lived my whole life.

"You need to let me know you hear me," Dad said. His voice still sounded like a growl, but I could also hear something else. Something like maybe he might start crying. I had never seen him cry, not even when Mom's father died.

"Yes, sir," I said. "I hear you."

Dad nodded. And he walked into the house. I braced myself for the sound of the screen door slamming but it didn't, which surprised me. Last I knew the little closer valve was in need of fixing. Maybe they'd already begun making little repairs, for whoever was going to live here after we'd gone.

When I finally got up from the picnic table myself, I noticed Dad had left his rifle there. I checked to make sure the safety was fastened and carried it on up to the barn. Not that I felt like helping him any. I just didn't want to give him and Mom more excuses than they already had to holler at one another.

Eleven

Weeks went by, unfolding into colder weather, and for the first time ever we did not have Thanksgiving at the farm. Instead Mom paid Trudy's niece to watch the horses, and we spent three days in Raleigh. Or should I say we spent three miserable days in Raleigh, because everyone was so stressed out that even nice, cheerful Holly snapped at my mother and my sweet, calm mother snapped right back, and Dad got right into it too, taking Holly's side. There's not much point going into the details. Suffice to say I had never been so happy to get home. Straightaway I called up Tim. He said he'd borrow his mom's car and come get me.

Dad came out while I was waiting with Daisy on the front stoop. "Where you going?"

"Riding around with Tim," I said.

He scratched his head a minute. If they hadn't been so

wrapped up in the farm, I'm sure my parents would have made Tim the topic of much discussion and warning and rules. But as it happened, they'd barely said a word.

Now Dad dusted off his old parenting skills. "I'm trying to remember when we said you could ride in cars with guys," he said.

"You never bothered saying I could or couldn't, but since I've been doing it for about three months, I'd say that ship has sailed."

Dad sighed. "Wren," he said, "I don't know when you got all grown up."

By now I could see Mrs. Greenlaw's shiny, clean car, getting all dirty from the dust in our driveway. I gave Daisy a scratch on her head and stood up. Dad looked tired, and I knew Thanksgiving had been even worse for him than it had been for me. It used to be that he and Mom got along just fine. The only thing they'd ever fought about was money, and now since the only thing anyone ever talked about was money, all they ever did was fight.

"Don't worry, Dad," I said, taking pity on him. "I'm not all grown up just yet."

He smiled and ruffled my hair. "Glad to hear it, Wrenny. Very glad indeed."

Tim got out of the car and came over to shake Dad's hand and talk to him a minute about what a safe driver he was, then we got into the car and drove away. Halfway down the road we switched so I could practice driving, even though technically Tim hadn't had his license long enough to count as a supervising driver. It made me feel kind of reckless and powerful, this little bit of lawbreaking.

On the way into Williamsport we passed the turnoff to Knockton Farms. I asked Tim if he'd mind stopping here a minute. It was the Saturday after Thanksgiving, so the place looked pretty deserted. I pulled in front of the barn and we walked on in. I checked out the horses in the stalls, but didn't find Brutus. It looked like a pretty nice place, though, smelling of clean straw and the same castile soap my mom and I used to clean tack.

"Can I help you two kids?" A lady in a T-shirt and chaps came into the barn, leading a saddled quarter horse. I felt my face go hot, like I'd been caught somewhere I shouldn't be. Tim noticed and spoke up for me.

"My friend here used to own a horse that you bought recently," he said. "She just wanted to visit him."

"Oh," said the lady. "You must be the Piner girl. Well, Brutus is doing just great."

"You didn't change his name?" I felt relief at this, along with her niceness.

"No, ma'am, I didn't. Brutus is out in that pasture by the silo." She jutted her chin in the direction. "You come on by and visit with him anytime you like."

"All right," I said. "Thank you. Does he mind it much, being ridden for lessons?"

"He seems to like it just fine," she said, in that same nice and understanding voice. I smiled at her, remembering how gentle Brutus had always been with my friends.

"Thank you," I said.

At the pasture, Tim and I climbed up on the wooden fence. I made a clucking noise and called out, "Brutus."

The thing about horses, they're fairly low-key as far as expressing affection. For example, if for some terrible reason we ever had to give Daisy away, and then I came to visit her, you can bet she would have knocked me over and smothered me with kisses. A horse won't do that. But what Brutus did was touching in its own way. He lifted his head like the sound of my voice had startled him. Then he let out a little rumbling snort and trotted over with his ears pointed toward me. When he got there, he arched his head over the gate and started chewing on my left pocket, where I generally kept sugar cubes.

"He missed you," Tim said.

"I missed him, too." These days, because of my hurt hand, I kept my sugar cubes in my right pocket. I reached in, pulled a couple out, and fed them to Brutus, glad that I could come see him whenever I wanted.

In town Tim and I ate lunch at a little Southern restaurant that Allie's parents used to take me to, so I guess I shouldn't have been surprised to see her mom there. Mrs. Hackett was eating a salad with a couple of her friends—probably other professors—and when she noticed me it reminded me of the way Brutus had acted. She did a little double take and then stood up and came zooming over to our table. But once she got there, she didn't hug or kiss me or anything; she just kind of reached out and touched my arm.

"Wren," she said. "I haven't seen much of you lately."

It was true. Especially compared to how it used to be. Last year at this time Allie still lived in Leeville, and we spent our lives at each other's houses. We saw each other as much as . . . well, as much as I saw Tim now.

I introduced her to Tim, and he stood up to shake her hand. Mrs. Hackett shuffled a little, like she wanted to say something but wasn't sure if she could say it in front of Tim. I could see her thinking, and working out how to put her words together. Finally she just said, "We miss you over at our house, Wren. I know Allie misses you too. I hope you'll come and see us soon."

"Yes, ma'am," I said.

Tim and I sat quiet a minute as she walked back to her table. Then Tim said, "I know she likes me, you know."

"Who?" I said, my cheeks instantly turning red. For a weird moment, even though he'd said "she," I thought he meant me.

"Allie." Across the room I thought I saw Mrs. Hackett

move her head a little, like she had this instinct for knowing when someone was talking about her daughter.

"You do?" I said.

"Yeah," he said. "I knew from the first day."

"Well," I said. "It's flattering, anyway." Tim shrugged in this way that admitted pretty much every girl he'd ever met in his life ended up with a crush on him.

"Remember that day I told you?" he said. "About me?"

"Not something I would forget," I said.

Tim took a bite of his sandwich. Then he said, "I thought about kissing you that day. Really kissing you, I mean."

"I knew it!" I said, and hit the table with the flat of my good hand. "I mean, I thought you were going to kiss me. And then you did!"

I expected him to laugh, but instead he looked very serious. "The thing is," he said, "I used to think I could get a girlfriend and that would solve everything. And I tried a couple times. But it didn't seem fair. You know? Does it seem fair to you?"

"No," I said. And in this wistful voice I hoped he couldn't read, I said, "I sure am glad you're not my boyfriend."

Tim nodded in agreement. Seeing that made my heart turn inside out—a painful, twisty feeling. He said, "You deserve a boyfriend who likes girls." I nodded, nodded, nodded, all the while thinking that as long as we could just go on like this together, the two of us, sharing secrets across the table, it was enough. At the same time, I remembered that couple I'd seen, pressed together at Wilbur Beach, and I knew it wasn't enough, not really.

"You know the whole thing about this new Lutheran church?" Tim said. "And that website and everything? It's saying there's no such thing as being gay, that all you have to do is decide to like girls. They've got this quote on there, saying, 'God loves gays but hates a perverted lifestyle.' It's not like I never tried—hell—I went out with Caroline Jones a whole year."

I really wanted to ask how far it had gone but couldn't quite figure out how to word it, never mind that it was none of my business. Tim said, "All the time I was going out with Caroline I tried my hardest to like her in the ways I was supposed to. But I couldn't do it. Meanwhile she liked me just the way she should, and it just seemed so unfair. Wrong to me. Doesn't it seem wrong to you?"

"It does," I said, wishing he would stop asking me that. "You shouldn't have to lie about how you feel or who you are."

Tim speared a piece of the fried okra we'd ordered. "But I *am* lying about it," he said. "I'm lying about it to everyone except you. And that's how they want me to live my whole entire life. They want me to marry some unsuspecting Lutheran girl and sit across the table from her every day of my life, sleep with her every night of my life, pretending I like her instead of someone else. Do you think that's right?"

"You know I don't," I said.

Tim smiled. But lately I had started to notice how his smiles were not so convincing anymore. The world had started to chip away at his natural cheerfulness. I wished there were something I could do besides listen. It was very weird to want two different things, but I had to admit I did. I wanted Tim not to be gay, so he could fall in love with me. And I also wanted the world to not mind that he *was* gay, so he could stop hurting so bad all the time. These two wishes sure seemed opposite from each other, and yet I went ahead and wished them both.

The next Monday I had another appointment with James to look at my hand. This time Mom came in with me. By now it had pretty much healed, though he said I would always have a big red scar in the middle of my palm. "I guess it's not the worst place to have a scar," I told him.

James, who saw all kinds of terrible scars and burns every day of his life, nodded. He said, "It may not seem like it, Wren, but you were lucky. Drinking and bonfires are a bad combination."

I reminded James, "I wasn't drinking."

"But the girl who bumped into you was," he said. He told us about a girl he'd treated last year who fell into a bonfire and had her hair catch on fire. It lit up and scarred both sides of her face. Hearing this, my mother put her hand over her heart and breathed in real hard. It seemed like she over-reacted to everything these days. Poor Mom.

"Your fingers look good," James said. "You can probably go back to playing guitar again."

Mom perked up at this. "Oh, good," she said. "I'll call Ry."

"Maybe I'll just pick it up at home for a bit," I said. "See how it feels."

"Okay," Mom said. I could tell she felt a little relieved at one less thing to pay for.

On the drive back to school, for no good reason, I thought about the conversation Tim and I had had at lunch on Saturday. And I couldn't help but wonder, with a little ball of fear forming in my gut, that maybe it wasn't just the church that had Tim thinking about being gay in practice versus gay in theory. Maybe he had started liking somebody. The idea made my heart do that inside-out thing again. At the same time I remembered his face in the library, and him saying he wanted to be dead and sounding like he meant it. I knew I couldn't keep Tim all to myself forever. Not when I wasn't enough to make him sure he wanted to keep on living.

"It wouldn't matter if I did like somebody," Tim said, because like the tactless idiot I am, I blurted out my whole thought process later that afternoon when we went for a horseback ride. It occurred to me in that moment that Tim and I talked about everything in the world except for how I felt about him. I wondered if he knew, if he could tell. The last thing in the world I wanted was him feeling like there was one more person in his life who expected him to be different than he was.

I'd put Tim on Sombero, who wasn't the calmest horse in the world, but my mom had trained him so well I thought it would be okay. It was a teensy bit cold, particularly since neither of us had worn our coats, but I didn't mind. The air felt crisp and clean, and Tim was real agreeable whenever I told him to hold his reins looser or put his heels down.

"Of course it would matter if you liked somebody," I said.

"No," Tim disagreed. "There's no way in hell I'd do anything about liking another guy while I'm living in Williamsport, North Carolina."

I reached down and petted Pandora. What Tim said made me feel relieved and worried all at the same time.

"Maybe I'll just be a priest or something," he added. "And just never have any kind of sex at all."

"But then you'd have to be Catholic," I said, as if that were the only problem with the priest plan.

"Can't be any worse than being Lutheran," Tim said. "As it turns out."

Sombrero stopped walking for no good reason. Tim pressed his heels in real gentle, just like a natural. His posture looked so good, you'd think he'd ridden a horse every day of his life. I thought what a great athlete he was, and how he'd already decided not to play baseball in the spring. And I realized I almost never saw Tim happy anymore, except for when he was up on the stage.

All through *Finian's Rainbow*, Og has this huge crush on Sharon, the main girl. But he also kind of likes Susan, coincidentally played by Caroline Jones. He sings this funny song called "When I'm Not Near the Girl I Love." In the end he sings this funny line, "For Sharon I'm carin', but Susan I'm choosin', I'm faithful to whos'n is here."

It was a good solution for Og, but choosing between two girls in a musical comedy is just not the same as choosing between girls and guys in your real life. Seeing the expression on Tim's face, I wondered how anyone in the world could think it *was*.

"You know," I said to my parents at dinner that night. "I've been thinking about homosexuality."

The three of us sat in the kitchen. Mom had heated up a Mrs. Budd's chicken potpie and I'd made a tossed salad, making the dressing I'd invented, with soy sauce because vinegar upset Dad's stomach. My parents looked at each other in a way I hadn't seen in a good long while. Like they'd had the same reaction to something and wanted to check in with each other.

"Have you," Dad said.

"I saw this website," I said, "that said all this stuff about homosexuality being a sin. And how it was a choice. But you know, if you think about other sins, like drinking and premarital sex and all that. Well, those are things that are naturally tempting to everybody. So, if you think that homosexuality is so naturally tempting that it needs resisting, well, you must be a homosexual yourself. So probably all those people who think gays are bad are just really gay themselves."

Mom laughed. "I've had that same thought, Wren."

Dad put down his fork and said, "It's just ignorant people looking for excuses to be hateful. That's all." He picked up his fork to start eating again, then paused. "Why were you looking at an antigay website, anyway?"

"Tim showed it to me," I said. "His church sent it to him. They're mad because gay people are allowed to be ministers."

Dad pushed his plate away like something very serious had happened. He said, in his sternest voice, "So is Tim trying to tell you that it's wrong to be gay?"

My father's face looked electric and somber at the same time, like a serious line had just been crossed. And I felt a surge of love. At the same time it seemed unfair that my parents felt this way when I didn't even need them to. It was hard to know what to say. In that moment I sure didn't feel like lying.

Just like in the old days—with her horses, and with Daisy, and with a hundred other things too—it was my mom who saved the day. "Joe," she said. "Tim doesn't think it's wrong to be gay. He doesn't think that at all. Does he, Wren?" I could tell from her face, looking all calm and understanding. All this time I wondered why she didn't know, she *did* know. She just knew better than to say anything.

"No, ma'am," I said. Being from the North, my mother doesn't usually expect me to call her ma'am. But in that moment I wanted to do some little thing that showed how much I respected her. "He sure doesn't think it's wrong to be gay."

"We get it," Mom said. "You don't need to say another word."

And everyone went back to eating.

Meanwhile, Allie wanted nothing to do with me. She started hanging out with a couple of kids who used to go to Cutty River, a girl named Ginny and also Jesse Gill. Part of me hoped Tim would notice that Allie was friends with Jesse, which would prove she was trustworthy and could be told the truth about us. Another, less generous part of me wanted things to continue exactly as they were, me with Tim— everyone including Allie thinking we were a couple—and Allie off with her new friends.

"I ran into Allie's mother today," Mom said to me one afternoon. We were in the barn, forking fresh hay into the stalls. Mom had adopted out two more horses, and I almost hated being in the barn as it emptied out one by one. At the same time I made myself go out there at least once a day, to make sure Pandora was still right where she belonged. I shoveled the last forkful of straw into her stall, then climbed in with her. I wrapped my arms around her neck and buried my face in her mane. Obviously Mom wanted to talk about Allie. If she'd wanted to talk about her mother, she would have just called her Julia.

Mom stuck her head into the stall and said, "She says Allie's been having a really hard time at Williamsport."

"Well," I said, "I haven't been seeing much of her these days."

"She said that, too."

"Mom," I said. "It's not like I've deserted her or anything." Then I felt super guilty saying that, because I guess I had deserted her.

"I know that, honey. It's just, things have been going well for you. Have you thought about that? You've made new friends, you've got Tim. You've got a part in the play. And for Allie, nothing has gone the way she imagined it. She feels lost."

I told Mom how Allie had acted when she found out about the farm.

"Maybe you just took her by surprise," Mom said. "People don't always say exactly the right thing when they hear bad news, you know. Especially fifteen-year-old people."

Pandora let out a soft nicker, like she agreed with Mom. I lifted up my face. "So what do you think I should do?"

"You should give her another chance," Mom said. "Obvi."

I rolled my eyes at Mom's attempt to be one of the girls, and she laughed. As if I would ever take her advice on how to handle my friends.

"Mom says I should give you another chance."

This might not have been the most tactful lead-in. Allie looked up from where she sat on the curb waiting for her bus—the early bus, since she didn't have an after-school activity. I figured I could get to rehearsal a little late. Our performance was coming up in just one week, so we'd been running straight through the play, and my song didn't come on till toward the end of Act 1.

"Funny," Allie said. She had a book open in her lap and looked back down at it instead of at me. "My mom says the same thing about you."

I sighed and sat next to her. She tapped her pencil on her book, like she felt impatient for me to leave. "Well," I said, "maybe we should both listen. We've been friends a long time, you know. And I'm really sorry you're having such a hard time."

At this her head shot up. She had her hair in a ponytail and had wiped the makeup off her face, so she looked more like the old Allie than I'd seen her in a long time. Not to sound like my dad, but she looked so much better this way. I wished she'd stop messing herself up with all that extra effort.

"Who says I'm having a hard time?" she said. "I'm not

having a hard time at all. Things are great. Really great. I'm so glad to be rid of Devon. And Ginny is a much cooler girl than I ever realized. She cracks me up every day. Jesse, too. And . . ." She started tapping her pencil again, and I could tell she was racking her brain for something else that was great.

"Okay," I said. "I'm glad you're not having a hard time."

"Thanks," she said. "So. Have you figured out where you're going to move?"

I stared at her for a minute. Her face looked tense and empty. If she cared about me at all, if she had any idea of what my family was going through, you sure couldn't see it from the way she acted.

"No," I said. "We haven't figured out where we're going to move. But thanks so much for asking." The bus pulled up with a great wheezing and hissing of brakes. Allie snapped her book shut and shoved it into her book bag.

"Well," she said. "Thanks so much for forgiving me. I really feel better now."

"You're welcome," I said.

We both stood up, and Allie marched past me. I watched her get onto the bus and thought about standing there until it pulled away, but what was the point? The only thing I could do to make Allie like me again was prove that Tim was not my boyfriend, and at this point that might not even do any good. And honestly, I couldn't think what she could do to make me feel better about her and the fact that she would dump me forever over a boy she'd barely ever spoken to. Which as far as I was concerned was just the beginning of things she'd done wrong. I decided then and there I was going to stop trying.

A small flock of Canada geese who couldn't be bothered migrating squawked as I walked past the retention pond. I thought of the old Allie, and all the fun times we'd had, and how we used to be able to talk about anything. It was hard not to wish for that girl back, because I had so much to tell her.

Twelve

My parents got an offer on the house. It came out of the blue because they hadn't officially been trying to sell it yet, but the lady from Knockton Farms told some rich friends how we were having trouble, and it turned out they'd been looking for a piece of property to buy for their son, who was a chef. He wanted a place near town with a big old house and a lot of land where he could cater weddings and such. There was all kinds of complicated information that I knew mostly from hearing my parents fight about it. Nobody told me anything directly, but what I gathered was that the offer was for way less than we owed on the house, so the bank had to approve it. It seemed to me that if the bank was willing to take less money than we owed, why not just reduce the amount we owed and let us keep it? But as I found out on a more and more regular basis, life just didn't work that way. Meanwhile Mom had brought our barn cats over to Knockton, but we still had ten horses and possibly a whole lot less time than we thought to figure out where we were going to flee to when all this finally ended.

Mom and Dad fought pretty much round the clock. Mom's face had turned this constant shade of red, and anytime I woke up during the night I could hear her rattling around the house—she'd pretty much stopped sleeping altogether. She'd also lost a whole lot of weight, while my dad—who had a tendency to eat under stress—put on about fifteen pounds. It was like the weight moved off her body and onto his.

To drown out the sound of their fighting, and because *Finian's Rainbow* was mere days away, I sang my "Necessity" song all the time. I couldn't wait to perform it onstage. In the play, Annie Leonard started out singing, "What is the curse that makes the universe so all bewilderin'?" Then I came in and sang, "What is the hoax that just provokes the folks they call God's children?" After that Elizabeth Claire Zimmerman sang, "What is the jinx that gives a body and his brother and everyone around the runaround?" And then we all sang "Necessity." I had one verse that I sang all on my own, my solo, and it went like this:

My feet want to dance in the sun
My head wants to rest in the shade
The Lord says go out and have fun
But the landlord says, "Your rent ain't paid!"

So you can see how in addition to being something I had to practice, the song felt relevant to our home life, to the point where one morning at breakfast Mom came right out and asked me to stop singing it. "At least all the time," she said, kind of apologetic, when she saw the hurt feelings on my face.

I felt like saying I'd stop singing when she and Dad stopped hollering at each other, but she looked so fragile that I bit my tongue. Mom was spending hours and hours on the telephone, trying to find other rescue groups to take her horses. But they all had the same problem: When people needed to start economizing, the first place they started was charitable donations. Especially charitable donations to animals. That morning Mom picked up the phone to start making her calls before I even left for school, and I'm sorry to say that she forgot to say good-bye to me.

Daisy walked me down to the end of the driveway and waited with me until the bus came. She was the only member of our family who didn't know what was going on, and I envied her.

We were going to have four performances of the play: Thursday night, Friday night, a Saturday matinee, and Saturday night. Each performance would be packed, because as I have said, people from all over the area came to Williamsport High productions.

As the week began I made a decision that nothing—not Allie scowling at me in American history, not my parents fighting, not even the fate of all our horses—would let me feel anything except excited about this being the week I performed in my first Williamsport High School play. Do you know how many other sophomores were singing solos? None, that's how many. And do you think my parents stopped for a single second to feel proud about this? No, they did not.

On Monday, after school but before rehearsal, I hung out for a bit on the stone wall by the football field with Tim, Caroline Jones, Tyler, Devon, Rachel, and Jay. Us girls and Tim sat on the wall, while Jay and Devon stood there wearing their football gear for practice. Rachel chatted away with Devon, looking like she couldn't believe her good fortune. I almost had a flash of sympathy for him when I thought how Allie had always saved her adoring glances for Tim. It was hard to blame him for dropping her for someone who actually liked him. Anyway, in the midst of our various conversations, Caroline happened to mention the cast party, which was going to be at her house.

"Are your parents going to be there?" Devon asked.

"Well, of course they are," Caroline said. "They're not going out of town the weekend I'm starring in the school play." Really Liza Jane Rawls, who played Sharon, was the star of the play, but I did not point this out to Caroline.

Devon frowned. "But they'll make themselves scarce, right?"

"What do you care?" Caroline said. "The cast party is for the *cast*, Devon, not the football team." A couple of those geese flew overhead, squawking away.

"Caroline Jones," Devon said, in a mock Southern accent. "You have been sitting there talking about a party in front of us for nearly five minutes. Are you telling me we aren't invited?"

Caroline turned a little pink. "Well, of course you can come," she said, pointedly looking at Jay and Rachel, too. "But my parents are going to be there, and if you're think-ing of drinking, that's your own business. I don't drink any-more." She looked over at me when she said this last part, and I found myself putting my hand over my palm. I hadn't even attempted to go to another party since the bonfire. But surely my parents wouldn't expect me to miss the cast party of my very first play? There wouldn't likely be a bonfire at Caroline's house, anyway. And I never did get around to telling them she was the one who pitched me into the fire.

On Thursday morning my aunt Holly called my cell phone while I was waiting for the bus.

"Hi, Wren," she said. "I'm just calling to say I can't come this weekend. I'm really sorry. You know I've been looking forward to seeing your play."

The bus pulled up at the end of our driveway. I got on

with the cell phone still to my ear, not answering Holly and barely nodding my head at Jim, the bus driver. Being rude to everyone, in other words. I walked all the way to the back of the bus to where Tim sat eating a packet of little powdered doughnuts. He moved his bag to make space for me.

"Wren?" Holly said. "Are you still there?"

"I'm here," I told her.

"Your dad said he'd videotape it for me," she said. "Not the whole thing, obviously, but your song."

"The school makes DVDs of the performances," I said. "You can buy one for ten dollars."

"Oh, great!" Holly said, like this solved everything.

"Great!" I imitated her singsong, cheerful voice. "Well, since that solves everything, I'll see you when I see you."

"Wren, wait," Holly said. She could tell I was about to hang up. "I know that doesn't solve everything. But things are so tense I really don't think it's a good idea for me to come. I love your mom so much, you know I do, and once this whole Hillsdale thing is settled—"

"Hillsdale thing?"

Now it was Holly's turn to go quiet. I sat there, listening, and even though she didn't so much as breathe, it was the loudest silence I had ever heard.

"What's Hillsdale?" I said, getting a little loud myself.

"Um . . . I think you should ask your parents, Wren. I didn't realize they hadn't said anything to you."

I racked my brain trying to think if the word "Hillsdale" had floated up from any of Mom and Dad's umpteen fights. Nothing. Clearly the name was loaded enough that even in the heat of fury they'd remembered to whisper it.

Then I thought of something. "Wait. I know what it is," I said, recalling the plan they'd come up with at the Indian restaurant. "It's a boarding school where Mom can teach riding. Right? We're moving there?"

This time I heard Holly take in a breath. "You might be," she said, leveling with me. Clearly now there'd be no convincing her to come to the play. My parents were going to kill her.

"And where is it?" I said. "Where is this boarding school?"

"New Hampshire," Holly said.

New Hampshire! It might as well have been Timbuktu. I turned off my phone and dropped it in my book bag. I wasn't trying to be rude. I just felt stunned. New Hampshire. I pictured mounds and mounds of snow. Classrooms filled with rich northerners just like Devon.

Tim handed me one of his tiny doughnuts. He had white powder across his chin, and I could see from his face that he understood, without asking, exactly what had happened. It was too bad Holly wouldn't come to *Finian's Rainbow*, because it looked like it could very well be my one and only play on the Williamsport High School stage. I closed my hand around that doughnut, put my head on Tim's knee, and just stared down the aisle of the bus, hardly moving the whole ride, and not saying a single word.

There was no time the rest of the day to feel sad, even over the complete and total ruination of my life. I had to go to classes, and the whole cast had lunch together in the auditorium, because Ms. Winters wanted to make sure we had light but protein-packed meals just like she'd told us. Of course I had packed my own. I didn't even know if my parents remembered that tonight was the first performance. I sure hadn't bothered reminding them.

As soon as the last bell rang, we all met for last-minute blocking and hair and makeup. I wore an old-fashioned dress with an apron over it and a kerchief in my hair, plus shoes with thick heels, since Annie and Elizabeth Claire were both about six inches taller than me. This didn't worry me. My voice was plenty big even if I wasn't.

If only I could take that first performance and bottle it up— keep it somewhere so that anytime I wanted I could just step right inside. Because for the first time in what seemed a million years—long enough to find an alligator and ship him off down further south, long enough for me to lose my old best friend and gain a new one, long enough to lose our horse farm to a catering business—none of those thoughts entered my head. All I saw was that pulsing, happy audience. Not their faces, which just looked like a million dots, but their applause and their attention. When I wasn't onstage I hid out in the wings, watching Tim sing his lines and dance with Caroline Jones. I felt so proud of both of them, Caroline dancing so prettily, and Tim so funny and charming, his voice sounding so strong and good. And we must have done a decent job with our "Necessity" song, because the whole audience got to their feet and gave us a standing ovation.

Reality didn't enter again till after the performance. Mom and Dad were waiting for me at the front of the auditorium, holding a huge bouquet of sunflowers, my favorite. They both had smiles on their faces, the first I'd seen in ages.

"Wren!" Mom said. Her face looked bright and lit up and happy. "You were so wonderful! You were perfect! Didn't I tell you that song was a showstopper?"

Dad had his hands shoved in his pockets. Despite being all pale and bloated, he looked almost like himself when he said, "Wren, you were just great. You sang that song so loud and pretty."

I took the flowers and let them hug me. "Did you see Ry was in the audience?" Mom said. "I thought he was going to stick around and say hi; I don't know where he went."

I shrugged. What in the world mattered less than Ry these days? I had a real life to worry about.

"Allie was here too," Dad said.

The exhilaration of the performance faded right before

my eyes, and the real world came crashing down. The word "Hillsdale" came into my head, but even I wasn't mean enough to throw it out at my parents just then. They still had the glow of the performance, even if mine had disappeared.

"Let's go home," I said. "I'm fried."

I barely got to see Tim in the shuffle. He was off with his parents and his sister, who'd come home from college to see the play. We waved to each other as we filtered through the crowd with our families.

On the drive home I told my parents about the cast party. I decided not to phrase it like a question. "Tim's going to have his mom's car, so you don't have to worry about driving me."

They both sat quiet, and I could tell they were agreeing without saying anything or even looking at each other, which reminded me of the way they used to be. Then Mom said, "You can go to the party with Tim, but we'll pick you up. At midnight."

"Midnight! The party won't even start till eleven!"

They were quiet again, that little telepathic back and forth.

"We'll pick you up at one, then," Mom said.

"But, Mom—"

"One thirty," Dad growled. "And that's my final offer."

I knew two things from his voice: He was willing to

compromise because I'd done so well in the play, and he wasn't willing to compromise a bit more than one thirty.

"Okay," I said.

"And in case you're wondering," Dad said, "I've still got that Breathalyzer."

Thirteen

Given what I'm about to tell you, it makes sense that this is chapter 13. Not that I'm a suspicious person. And probably you're thinking, what more bad luck could there be? Or maybe I've got it all wrong, and you think that I've spent a lot of time whining about nothing. I mean, apart from Allie, and the farm, things had been going just fine for me at Williamsport High.

In addition to the farm, though, the "apart from Allie" was a big deal. Please don't think I didn't have feelings about that, because I did. I would see her across the room with her new best buddy, the two of them all dolled up (Ginny had taken to outfits and makeup just like Allie), and I would feel this combination of jealousy and sadness. You can't have a best friend your whole life and not feel like you lost something when she's gone.

Plus, the fact that I was loving Williamsport High made

the fact that I probably wouldn't be able to stay so much harder. Those three days of performing *Finian's Rainbow* were the best and worst of my life all at the same time. Because I felt so alive; I felt *successful*. And at the exact same time I knew it wouldn't last, because I was about to get yanked right on out of it all.

But truth be told, the worst thing, the thing that's about to happen, didn't even happen to me. And maybe it had been a long time coming, and maybe things would turn out okay after it happened—a darkest-before-the-dawn scenario. At the time, though, it just seemed like about the most awful luck a person could have. Worse than losing your best friend, or your career in high school theater, or even your farm. It felt like the absolute end of the world.

Before it all blew up, before it got to a point where we—pretty much everyone I've been talking about so far—had to admit that nothing would ever be the same again, life went on just revolving around the play. One thing I knew: Wherever I ended up, I wanted to keep acting in plays. It made me sad not to be able to tell Allie this. If we'd still been friends, we could have hatched a plan to spend a year in New York after high school. She could be a model and I could try out for plays. Or maybe I could go to drama school. But of course that wasn't going to happen now, because here we both were in North Carolina, never saying a single word to each other.

But I didn't think about that on Friday, and I surely didn't think of it on Saturday when we had two performances. Every performance went better than the one before, and on Saturday night—the last performance—when I stood up there for my curtain call holding hands with Annie and Elizabeth Claire, I concentrated on soaking up every single clap from the audience, and every single whistle and hoot.

Then the lights came up, and everything kind of washed over me. A sadness—like the best moment of my life had passed and here I was, only sixteen years old, with nothing good to look forward to.

"What are you talking about?" Tim said, when I told him this. We were standing in the middle of everybody in the auditorium, all our cast mates along with people in the audience who'd come to tell us how great we were. It was so loud that I could tell him something like that in his ear, about how I felt, and not worry that anyone else would hear me.

"You can try out for *A Midsummer Night's Dream,*" he said. Ms. Winters had told us that would be the spring production and everyone had groaned, but I already had my copy from the library. Even if I got a part, it just wouldn't be the same. Nothing would ever be the same, I felt sure of it.

By now pretty much everyone who had to tell me I did a good job had already done it, and Tim—being one of the main stars—still had a lot of well-wishing to get through, so I broke out of the crowd to go say good-bye to my parents, who were sitting together in the back row. I guess it's only fair to mention that they came to every single performance, and also bought DVD copies for themselves and Aunt Holly.

"You're probably tired of us telling you how fabulous you were," Mom said, as I came up to them. I shrugged. I sure didn't feel like telling them how down I felt and almost wanted to say that I'd come home with them and skip the party. My hand throbbed a little, like it was remembering what happened the last time I had a big social event.

But I didn't ask to go home. I just kissed them both, and they reminded me that they'd be picking me up at one thirty on the dot, and if I wasn't waiting for them on the front porch, they'd come on in after me. Dad tried hard to sound stern when he said this, but his voice couldn't shake that giddy sound of pride. Instead of making me happy, it was just one more thing that seemed depressing.

Tim and I drove to the party just the two of us, which felt kind of like a miracle, since there'd been so many people mobbing him. He looked so happy it sort of lifted my spirits. These last few days he had been in the same boat as me, on this temporary high on account of the play. The difference was that he didn't seem to be experiencing any kind of let-down; he looked more like his old happy self. We didn't talk about anything serious, we just joked around, and luckily, his good spirits were contagious. By the time we pulled into

Caroline Jones's driveway, the two of us were singing songs from the play at the top of our lungs.

Of course Tim knew the way to Caroline's house, and I thought it was nice that the two of them had become friends again. I tried to picture what that relationship had been like. It turned out that Tim got off pretty scot-free, because Caroline had broken up with him to go out with Tyler. That didn't last much longer than last summer (I think she and Tyler broke up right after my hand-in-the-fire incident), but Tim got to take the high road. The only thing Caroline had ever said to me about the time they'd spent together was that Tim was always a perfect gentleman. I took that to mean he never pressured her to have sex.

Anyway: Caroline lived in this part of town called Woods Hill. It was one of the oldest sections of Williamsport, and the houses were grand and stately. Caroline's was a big white one with columns and a circular drive. I could guess just by looking at it that they had a pool in the backyard and her parents never, ever had to fight about money. I could feel my spirits sink right back down to where they'd been.

"Cheer up, Necessity Girl," Tim said, as he parked his mom's car on the street. I blushed, guessing he could read my mind, which he probably could. It was kind of funny— that Tim and I had become almost like my mom and dad, always knowing what the other was thinking. At the same time, I didn't like that I'd become the kind of person who got mad just seeing someone else's nice home. But it sure was hard to be happy about it when you were about to lose your own!

Don't ask me how so many people got to Caroline's house before we did. The front hallway was packed. Tim and I took off our coats and threw them into a room off the side of the foyer, a little den with a couch and desk. I'd had time to wash the makeup off my face, and wore jeans and a T-shirt under a cardigan sweater, my hair in a ponytail. Tim hadn't had much luck wiping off his Og makeup; he still had kind of a greenish tinge around his jawline. Even if you hadn't seen the play, you'd know all the cast members from their dampish hair and shiny faces. Everybody looked exhilarated, like we had all this leftover adrenaline and didn't know how to get rid of it.

I made my way to the kitchen and introduced myself to Caroline's mother. She stood at the stove ladling out mugs of eggnog (unspiked, of course), but I couldn't see drinking anything so heavy, so I got a bottle of water from a big cooler. Through the kitchen's sliding glass doors I could see just what I'd imagined—a great big glistening pool. In December, even in North Carolina, nobody would go swimming. But they had floated these pretty little candles on top of fake lily pads, and lots of kids stood around it talking. I had thought Tim was right behind me, but now I saw him out by the pool saying hey to Devon and Jay. Devon reached into his jacket and handed Tim some kind of bottle, which I guessed was whiskey. Tyler walked up, and Tim laughed at something he said, then took a giant swig.

Mrs. Jones told me I had a lovely singing voice. "Thank you, ma'am," I said. "Caroline sure is a wonderful dancer."

Mrs. Jones beamed. "She started ballet when she was three, but she was practically dancing before she could walk."

"I'll bet," I said.

"Caroline tells me you're Tim's new girlfriend?"

I had no idea what to say but opened my mouth anyway. Then closed it. Mrs. Jones laughed. "I wasn't trying to embarrass you, honey. We just love Tim around here. He's such a gentleman."

Right now I could see the gentleman out by the pool, taking another big swig of whiskey. Like me, plenty of the kids here were allowed to come to this party because Caroline had promised her parents would be here. I didn't know where Mr. Jones had stationed himself, but I knew then and there that two parents were no match for the steady stream of teenagers filing in.

"Thank you, Mrs. Jones," I said. "I sure like Tim too."

She went back to handing out eggnog, and I slid out the glass door and headed toward the pool. For a second I wished I'd gone back to get my jacket. It wasn't freezing, but cold enough that the breeze gave me goose bumps, even under my sweater.

"Hey, Necessity Girl," Tim said, when I walked up. He put his arm around me. I could tell from the way he leaned into me that he'd already had several sips of whiskey.

"Hey there, Og," I said.

Devon held his little glass bottle out toward me. I admit I was kind of curious and hated to seem like a goody-goody. But I remembered that sip of whiskey from the night at the bonfire, gagging and spitting it out. Thanks but no thanks. Anyway, the barest smell of it on my breath and I'd be grounded for the rest of my life. I shook my head.

"What a good girl," Devon said, in this half-mocking tone that almost made me not want to explain myself. Still, I didn't seem to be able to keep from talking, so while Tyler reached over and took the swig that had been offered to me, I told them about how strict my parents were about that sort of thing.

"Man," Jay said. "That's rough." He looked like he'd also had more than a few sips off Devon's bottle. His lips looked red, and so did his cheeks, even though he was wearing his big, thick varsity jacket.

"You look nice and cozy in that jacket," I said.

He immediately did the Southern gentlemanly thing by taking it off and putting it over my shoulders. As I slipped my arms into the lined leather sleeves, I caught sight of Allie, across the pool, glaring. It would have surprised me to see her if half the school hadn't been filing into Caroline's front hallway. I could see Mrs. Jones through the kitchen door, glugging eggnog into the big pot on the stove. Her efforts might have proved more useful elsewhere, because clearly Devon was not the only guest handing out liquor.

Allie came over to us with her new best friend, Ginny. They were both pretty dressed up, wearing makeup, and I suddenly felt self-conscious about my naked face and Old Navy jeans. I pulled Jay's jacket around me a little closer.

"Well, hey there," Devon said to Allie. He held out his bottle of whiskey, or whatever it was. To my surprise she grabbed it and took a giant swig.

"Whoa there," Devon said. "Slow down, little lady."

Ginny laughed, and after a second swig, so did Allie. "So where's Rachel?" she said to Devon, refusing to look over at Tim or me.

"Right over there," Devon said. He jutted his chin toward a cluster of cheerleaders, a few feet away. You can better believe Rachel had her eyes right on Allie and Devon, and I admired her for not rushing directly over.

Allie stared right back at Rachel, then took another sip of the whiskey, which she still hadn't handed back. Ginny reached over, took the bottle, and tried a sip of her own, but it looked pretty dainty. Even so she scrunched her nose up in a way that you knew she wouldn't be reaching for that bottle again.

"Hey, Allie," Tim said. His voice sounded different than usual, like there was a rubber band around his tongue. "Aren't you going to congratulate your friend Wren?"

Everybody was quiet for a minute. Allie looked over at me quickly, then looked away. Then she said, "Tim, I thought *you* were so funny and great. I about died laughing when you sang that 'Something Sort of Grandish' song."

"But what about Wren?" Tim said. He grabbed hold of my sleeve and pulled me closer to him. "What about sweet little Wrenny, your best friend? Don't you think she sang so pretty? Wasn't she great?"

"Yeah," Allie said. She must have heard how insincere this sounded because she added, in a perkier voice, "You did a good job, Wren."

"Thanks," I said. The whiskey bottle went around one more time. By the time it got back to Allie, there was only about one gulp left.

"Bottoms up!" Devon said. "I have another one in the car."

Allie threw back her head and finished off the bottle. I hoped Mrs. Jones couldn't see her through the glass door, because she didn't bother being subtle about it.

Devon headed out to the car to get that other bottle, and Allie, Ginny, and Rachel all went along with him.

*   *   *

More and more people were filing into the party. So much for Caroline saying it was just for the cast. It seemed like every teenager in Williamsport showed up, lounging around by the pool, laughing and yelling and sneaking drinks. Nobody seemed to worry much about getting caught, I guess with good reason, because Mrs. Jones went up to bed around midnight. I never did see Mr. Jones.

At some point I lost sight of Tim. Annie, Elizabeth Claire, and I settled in by the pool, crossing our legs on the dry deck because it was too cold to put our feet in the water. Caroline came over and sat down next to me.

"Wrenny," she said. "How are you doing?"

She sounded about as drunk as she'd been at the bonfire party, and someone yelled, "Don't let her knock you in the pool, Wren."

"At least I know how to swim," I yelled back, and everybody, including Caroline, laughed. Then she held out a bottle of some kind of clear liquor and offered me a sip.

"She can't," Allie said. "She never does." I don't know where she came from, but there she was, kind of swaying over the four of us. Allie went on, telling them in this snotty voice about how overprotective my parents were, and how my dad might or might not have a Breathalyzer. I had actually already told them all this myself, so I just sat there, staring at her, trying to think of something to say that would sound nice enough for her to start acting like her old self.

I didn't get a chance, though, because she put a hand to the side of her cheek, like she suddenly had a headache. Then she kind of teetered off away from us, toward the bushes. She looked so unsteady I figured I'd better follow her, but then I saw Ginny chasing her down.

"Who was that girl?" Caroline said. She didn't say it in a nice way. I could understand that, based on how Allie had behaved, but I just didn't have the heart to join in any meanness toward her.

"Allie," I said. "We used to go to the Cutty River School together." It felt strange to say this instead of what I'd called her since I could remember: my best friend.

I braced myself for whatever they were going to say next, but apparently Allie had worn herself out as a conversation topic. Tyler came over and sat down next to me. He gave me a little hug, but the person he looked at was Caroline. "Where's your boyfriend?" Tyler asked me, looking right over my head into her eyes. Like he didn't really want to know where Tim was, he just wanted me to get out of the way and go and find him.

"Well, hello to you too," I said. I stood up, and he smiled and flashed me the peace sign, then scooted right next to Caroline and told her how much he liked her dancing.

"Thanks, Tyler," she said. "I thought you rocked it too."

I decided to do what my gut told me I ought to, which was go check on Allie. It turned out she was busy puking in the bushes. Ginny fluttered around her, looking worried.

"She's supposed to sleep over," Ginny whispered. "But I can't bring her back like this. My parents will kill me."

Allie wiped her mouth and muttered something impossible to understand. Then she staggered away from us a bit and slid to the ground, leaning against the pool fence. Ginny and I followed her, mostly to put some distance between us and the puke.

"Can't you sneak her up to your room?" I said.

"I live just three doors down," Ginny said. "So we can walk home, but my Dad makes me ring the doorbell so he can see what state I'm in."

"Well," I said. "Maybe since you're not drunk he'll have mercy?"

"You don't know my father," Ginny said. "He'll tell Caroline's parents. He'll tell Allie's. And he'll ground me for three months just for being near her."

I thought about this. My parents would be plenty mad too. But they'd appreciate that I was stone-cold sober, and they'd want me to help out a friend. You can bet they'd tell Allie's parents, but they wouldn't necessarily get Caroline's involved. And they probably would wait till morning and have a talk with Allie, before calling her mom and dad.

So I made a decision. "She can come home with me," I said. "My parents are picking me up"—I looked at my cell phone— "in about twenty minutes." Wow, how could it be so late already?

"The hell I will," Allie said. "Goddamn traitor."

"Allie," I said. A smarter person would probably not have responded, given how drunk she was. But I went ahead and said, "Just how am I a traitor? Just how did I betray you, ever?"

"You stole my boyfriend!" she yelled, loud enough so that about four conversations stopped, heads swiveling to look at us.

I whispered as fiercely as I could. "I did not steal anyone! And he was never your boyfriend." After I said this I glanced around, trying to locate Tim. It had been about an hour, at least, since I'd seen him.

"He would have been if it weren't for you," Allie said. "I'm not going anywhere with *you*."

"Well," I said. "Sorry to tell you, you don't have much choice. Ginny won't bring you home. So it's either come with me or we'll have to call your mother to come get you right now."

"No, no." Allie's head had started kind of lolling to the side. "I'm fine," she insisted. "I'm just going to sleep a minute."

Ginny and I pulled her to her feet. She felt like she only weighed about four pounds, nothing but bone and air. We led her out to the front porch, where she slumped against the column and fell right to sleep. I sat next to her. Ginny couldn't get out of there fast enough. She barely even said good-bye to Allie, though she did give me a pretty passionate thank-you. Somebody had turned the porch light off, and I couldn't see anything on the front lawn except the moon shadows of the live oaks and the weeping willow. I was glad I still had Jay's coat on and hoped he wouldn't mind me wearing it home. Poor Allie must've been cold. She didn't have any jacket at all.

She started to say something, and for a second I thought she was talking to me. Then I realized she was just muttering incoherently. I moved over a little bit in case she was going to puke again. From down the street a pair of headlights came heading toward Caroline's house. I took out my cell phone and checked the time again. 1:25 a.m. Shoot. I hadn't even figured out what I was going to say to them about Allie. But I knew it would be a good idea to give them a heads-up. I stood up and jogged down the driveway a bit, so I could tell them before they got their first glimpse of her.

As our car pulled up, I peered into the passenger window. Phew. It was my mom, come to pick me up by herself. She was much less likely to storm the party than my dad.

"Hey, Mom," I said.

"Hey, Wren," she said. "Did you have fun?"

"I did," I said. She looked so much happier than she had in weeks; I hated to have to tell her about Allie. When I did, her face didn't fall. She just said, "Get in." When I slid into the seat next to her, she leaned in and took a good, deep whiff of my breath. I couldn't help it. I laughed. She laughed too.

"You sure don't smell like you've been drinking," she said.

"Because I haven't," I said. "Not a drop." She didn't look quite convinced, so I said, "You could make me recite the alphabet backward."

"That never seemed like a fair test to me," she said. And we both tried to do it as she pulled up the circular drive, without a whole lot of success.

There sat Allie, slumped on the porch. The lights from our car illuminated half the front yard. So that we could see, my mother and I, that Tim and Jay were standing in the middle of the front lawn, kissing. Not just kissing, but making out. Jay had his hands under Tim's shirt, and they were pressed together. Let me tell you that it's no fun to see the boy you love kissing someone else. Male or female. Still, it would have been more or less inconsequential if it had just been my mom and me—Allie being too out of it to notice anything.

But at the exact second we saw Tim and Jay in the bright light—moments before our car would have pulled in front of the house and blocked the sight of them—who should come walking out of the house but Devon and Rachel, along with two other girls I didn't know. Rachel's cheerleader friends.

"Oh no," I said.

"You get Allie," Mom said, instantly understanding. She turned off her headlights, but it was a little late for that. "I'll get the guys."

From the swift and expert way my mom moved, you would have thought Tim and Jay were a pair of thoroughbreds loose in somebody's meadow. She flew out of the car and to the middle of the lawn and guided them into our backseat. It took me slightly longer to get Allie up off the porch. I pushed her into the passenger seat next to my mom and climbed in back with Tim and Jay. To my mom's credit, she didn't peel out, though I could see her hands shaking on the steering wheel. She just eased that car down the driveway, while the hooting and shouting of drunken witnesses rose up behind us. I heard glass shatter, like someone had chucked a bottle at us. But I didn't turn around and look. I didn't want to give them the satisfaction of my worried face, peering back at them. And believe me, my face must've looked plenty worried.

"Well," my mother said, as she drove carefully up Woods Hill Road. "Can you introduce me to your friend, Wren?"

Obviously she knew Allie and Tim, so I said, "This is Jay. Jay, this is my mom." I shrugged out of the jacket and handed it to him. He took it without looking at me, just folded it up in his lap. From the way Jay and Tim sat, staring straight ahead with their hands on their knees, you would have thought they were riding in the back of a police car.

"Can I drop you at home, Jay?" my mother said.

"Yes, ma'am," Jay said. His voice sounded so deep, he could have been a sports announcer. "Thank you, ma'am," he added, and he gave her directions. Turns out he lived only a few blocks away.

My mom made sure Jay was safely in his front door, then headed toward Tim's house. Tim sat beside me, still staring straight ahead. He looked like a wax statue of himself. It scared me, seeing his face like that. I wanted to grab him, shake him, snap him out of it. I wanted to yell, "Tim! It doesn't matter! Can't you see? It doesn't matter one bit!"

But of course it did matter. I felt sick to my stomach, imagining what the kids would be saying at the party. If only there were some way for me to protect him, from everything. If only we could take him home with us, where I could watch him every second—and make sure that he'd be okay, and know that he was fine, and loved.

I reached over and grabbed hold of his hand. Tim clasped mine tightly, so tightly that the scars from my burn began to ache. But I didn't pull my hand away, just let him hold it so that my bones crunched, all the way to Cutty River Landing.

Fourteen

When I opened my eyes the next morning, I had that feeling you get when something terrible has happened—something that changes everything—but for a moment you can't quite remember what. There was just a hollowed-out place in my chest where nerves jangled into one another, jittery and off balance.

Then I remembered, the single image, the one everyone would take away from that party whether they'd seen it or not: Tim and Jay, kissing. I closed my eyes. *Tim.* Was he awake, too? What must he be feeling and thinking? I threw my feet over the side of the bed so fast that Daisy, who'd been sleeping at the foot of my bed, sat up, her face alarmed and ready for action. My whole body buzzed with this need to get to Tim as fast as humanly possible. I didn't know if there was any good I could do, but I needed to try; I needed to *see* him and know that he was all right.

The morning light made everything too bright as I rooted through my drawers for clothes. Daisy still sat at attention, watching me. Despite feeling very urgent, I tried to be quiet so as not to wake Allie, who was asleep on the twin mattress that I pulled out from under my bed when friends spent the night. Her mouth was wide open, and a string of spittle fell out onto the pillow. I had woken up to see her on that mattress a thousand times. By now she had grown way too long for it—the heels of her feet rested on the carpet, on almost the exact same spot she'd spilled paint when we were decorating the nesting dolls I'd gotten for my eighth birthday. She wore a gigantic denim shirt of my dad's that Mom and I had wrestled her into last night because her clothes reeked of whiskey and puke. Splayed out on that old twin mattress, Allie looked like the same best friend I'd had my whole life. I imagined how *she'd* feel when she opened her eyes. Poor Allie.

But between the two of them, Tim needed me more. Daisy thumped off the bed and followed me downstairs. My mom sat at the kitchen table, holding a mug of coffee and staring into space. I could tell she'd already gone for a morning ride: Her hair was in a braid and she smelled like horse sweat, which may sound to you like a negative thing but is actually quite nice.

"Hi, Mom," I said.

"Hi, Wrenny."

I reached in front of her and pulled an apple from the fruit bowl. Almost no humans in our house ever ate apples; we kept them for the horses. "I thought I'd go for a ride," I said. "Allie's still sleeping."

Mom nodded. "Leaving me to deal with her on my own, eh?"

"Well," I admitted, "I really want to go see how Tim's doing."

She smiled, but a sad smile. "Okay, Wren," she said. "We haven't even taken you for your driving test, have we? If we had, you could drive over."

"It's okay," I said. "It's more fun to ride, anyway."

She nodded, like that was the end of the conversation, but then just as my hand started to turn the doorknob, she said, "You're a good friend, Wren."

I let my hand drop to my side and turned around. "You're a good mother," I said. She looked at me like I had gone crazy. "No, really," I said. "I mean it. I'm serious."

"I can see that," she said. "I just didn't expect to hear those words from you. At least not during the troubled teenage years."

I smiled at her. I hope she could tell how grateful I was for how she'd acted last night, and how thankful I felt, because all I could manage to do was mutter, "Thanks," and head on out the door.

* * *

As soon as I rode Pandora through the open gate at Cutty River Landing, I wished I'd ridden my bicycle instead. What was I thinking? Pandora's hooves clip-clopped loudly on the paved road, past the swimming pool and all the brick houses that looked more or less the same. They all had giant SUVs, or Volvo station wagons, or shiny black Lexuses parked out front. I wondered how people weren't always walking through the door of the wrong house. All the lawns were perfect, and I prayed that Pandora wouldn't poop, even though these were exactly the sort of people who paid loads of money for bags of fertilizer over at Agway.

Tim's mother was standing out front hosing down the car that must've belonged to Tim's dad. She shaded her eyes as I came toward her, looking a little alarmed, and then she pasted on a smile when she realized it was me.

"Well, look at you, little cowgirl," she said. "I'm sorry to tell you, your friend Tim is in a world of trouble."

My heart stopped. Despite a little bit of grimness around her mouth, Mrs. Greenlaw looked mostly cheerful. Could she possibly know about Tim and Jay? I didn't dare say a word.

"How about you, Wren?" she said. "Did you get in trouble for drinking last night?"

"No, ma'am," I said.

I tried to think of some little joke I could make, but before I had a chance, she turned off the hose and said, "At least Tim had the good sense not to drive in that state." I guessed Tim hadn't told her it was my mom who brought him home. "He's inside getting ready for church," she went on. "I'll go get him for you. You'll have to stay here with your horse; we don't have a hitching post." She laughed as she wound the hose back on its little hanger and went inside to get Tim. I sat there on Pandora, not sure what to do, feeling kind of stupid. Pandora strained her head down toward the grass. I wasn't sure whether they'd thank me for the extra mowing, so I gave the reins a little tug and pulled her back a few steps.

Tim came out of the house wearing a coat and tie, his surfer blond-hair flopping across his forehead. From a distance he almost looked like his normal, handsome self, but as he walked close I could see his face was pale. Really pale. Even his freckles seemed washed the color of sand, and his eyes were bloodshot.

"Hey, Wren," he said. He reached out and petted Pandora's neck.

"Hey," I said. "I came by to see how you were doing."

He nodded, still looking at the horse instead of me. I had this feeling that if he said anything at all, he would lose it. To tell you the truth, I was about to lose it too. For a lot of reasons.

The only thing I could think to say was, "I think Jay is a nice guy."

Tim stopped petting the horse. He looked at me like I'd

gone crazy. "That's the last thing in the world I expected you to say."

"Well," I said, "I just think it's nice when someone you like likes you back." I tried not to let my voice crack, because how would I know?

"You see things in a funny way, Wren," Tim said.

"I think it's the way most people see things. It's just the people who think different are a whole lot louder."

"That's unfortunate," he said. "I get to spend an hour listening to the loud ones in about five minutes."

"I could save you," I said, hoping he could hear from my voice, I was only half-kidding. "You could climb right up on the horse with me and we could gallop away."

He leaned his head into Pandora's neck, like I had done a million times. She nibbled the collar of his jacket. I hoped against hope that it made him feel at least a little bit better.

"Well," I said, when I could tell he wasn't going to say anything, let alone run away with me. "Come on over to the farm after church, if you want."

I wish I had climbed down off my horse to give him a hug. But instead I just waved. He waved back, and I rode off through that brick-house world, lonesome and powerless.

When I got home, Mom and Allie were sitting at the kitchen table. Allie had a hot drink. It must have been tea or cocoa, because like me she didn't drink coffee. She still wore my dad's denim shirt, and I could hear the dryer tumbling away with her clothes from last night.

"Hey," I said to Allie. "How are you feeling?"

She let out this dramatic little groan. "Like I'm about to die."

"How's Tim?" Mom asked. I shrugged.

"Did he get wasted too?" Allie asked. Mom and I glanced at each other.

"Is your mom coming to get you?" I said, changing the subject.

"In an hour," Allie said. "After which I will be grounded for the rest of my life."

"Well then," I said. "Maybe we better take a walk while you still have your freedom."

Allie's clothes had dried. She pulled on her jeans and shirt and put my dad's shirt back on over it. Her hair looked lank and still smelled faintly of vomit, but she'd washed her face, and though her eyes looked narrow with exhaustion, I thought she looked prettier than I'd seen her in a long time, even if she didn't smell very good.

We walked up to the top of the west ridge. Most of the trees had gone bare, and you could see a whole lot of Leeville, the way it switched back and forth between farms and little suburban neighborhoods. I squinted toward Cutty River Landing, trying to pick out Tim's house, but the whole development just looked like a far-away Lego set.

Allie sat down on the ground. "I can't even believe how terrible I feel," she said. "My head is pounding, my insides feel just raked out. I really would want to die if I thought I was going to feel this way more than a day."

"Allie," I said. "Something happened last night."

Her eyes widened with horror. "Oh my God. What did I do?" She put her hands over her mouth and waited. For a second I felt a flare of anger, like why did she immediately make it about her? Then I thought about how scary it must be, not remembering what you'd done the night before.

"No," I said, deciding to forget the mean things she'd said to me, not to mention puking in the bushes. "It's about Tim."

I took a deep breath and reminded myself that it wasn't a secret anymore. I could say it out loud. And I wanted Allie to hear it from me—hear about Tim and Jay—before she heard it in a much uglier way.

"Something you don't know about Tim," I said.

She didn't react much, just a little twitch at her jaw as she stared up at me, listening. It felt too bizarre to just come and say the words, *He's gay*. So instead I told her about when Tim told me himself. Her eyes got kind of wide, and I hurried ahead and told her what had happened last night, how Tim and Jay were kissing, and how Devon and his friends saw. Listening to the words come out of my mouth, after all this time, I couldn't quite believe I was saying them.

By now Allie's hands sat flat on her knees. She stared wide-eyed, the color coming back into her face. After a long while she said, "God. I feel like such an idiot."

"Well," I said, not able to let this opportunity go by, "that's because you are an idiot."

She ratcheted out a little tuft of brown grass and threw it at me. Since the grass didn't weigh anything, it only traveled half an inch or so, landing just shy of her toe. We both laughed, then fell serious.

"Poor Tim," Allie said, and I nodded. Then she said, "Wren, I know I owe you an apology. Even if it weren't for all this—even if he really was your boyfriend—I owe you an apology. I had no right to just declare he was mine. I don't even know him."

It surprised me that Allie would say this first. "It's okay," I told her.

"It's not okay," she said. "I've been a terrible friend. You've been going through so much, with the farm and everything, and I've just been pouting about nothing."

"You've been going through a lot too," I said. "I know this year hasn't gone exactly the way you pictured it."

Now, all this might sound very mature. It might sound

like a grand reconciliation. But to my ears our voices did not quite match the words we were saying. Maybe in Allie's case it was on account of her hangover. I knew I should go over and sit beside her, that we should hug or something. But I felt a kind of hangover too, even though I hadn't had a drop to drink. It seemed like we both needed to just get the words out. We could deal with whatever we felt—if we ever felt anything—later.

From where I stood I could see Allie's mom driving down Cutty River Road and turning into our driveway. "Your mom's here," I said.

She dropped her face in her hands and groaned. "I just can't even tell you," she said, "how much I am not looking forward to seeing that woman."

I laughed and drummed my fingers on top of her head lightly. "It'll be okay," I said. And I knew the words were true as far as Allie was concerned. The person I didn't feel so certain of – as far as being okay—was Tim.

OMG, read the text from Caroline Jones, when I finally picked up my phone after Allie and her furious mother had driven away. IS IT TRUE?

I guess she wasn't really looking for confirmation, because when I called her back, the first thing she said— without even saying hello—was, "No wonder he never pressured me about sex."

"How did you find out?" I said.

"How did I find out? Rachel and her friends came right back inside, and the news spread like wildfire. Rachel even posted it as her Facebook status."

"What? How can that even be?" What a jerk! I knew I never liked that girl.

"She said something kind of mysterious about never judging a book by its cover, but then of course there were a million comments with people talking about what happened."

I wasn't allowed to have a Facebook account. But I could just imagine what this looked like, and it made me sick. I wondered if Tim was still at church, if he knew yet.

"Did Devon say anything?" I asked her.

"No," Caroline said. "But he didn't stop anyone from saying anything either. Poor Tim."

I said, "This should be an awesome day for him. After the play and all."

"I know," Caroline said. "The world is a very sucky place."

I hung up the phone and tried to think about whether this was true—about the world, that is. The buzzing, gnawing worry in my gut, about Tim and how he must be feeling, seemed to confirm that it was.

That afternoon he didn't call or come over even after hours ticked by and church must have finished. I flopped across my bed, thinking selfish thoughts about how come Monday everyone would know Tim wasn't really my boyfriend, and the play was over, so what would I have left? As I may have mentioned before, I can be quite a terrible person.

Daisy jingled into the room and got up on the bed with me, snorting dog breath in my face, but I barely had the heart to pet her. I kept picturing Tim's face as he'd petted Pandora, with the light gone out of it. Like someone had died. Pretending to be his girlfriend had been fun, I admit, but it had also worn on my heart, because all the while I knew it could never be real. But at least it was one way I could help protect him from the world, protect him from exactly what was happening now. And I guess a little part of me felt like if I couldn't do that for him, not only would he be at the world's mercy, but I'd lose him for good. My best friend, my fake boyfriend, the cutest boy in the whole school. Come tomorrow I would just be another girl, one whose bankrupt parents were about to lose the farm, literally.

Worse than that, a million times worse, what about Tim? What would happen to him now that everybody knew? It was the thing in the world that scared him most, and now it had come true.

Daisy gave up on me and lay down on the bed with a sigh. I wished again that Tim was right here in my room so I could see for myself that he was all right. But since he wasn't, I just lay across my bed, and I cried and cried, wishing there were something I could do—something real—to help him.

Fifteen

By the time Monday morning came around, I worried so hard I couldn't stand it. I had called and texted Tim a million times, asking if he could come over, or if I could go over there, and he only answered once, with a text that said in all capitals, NOT A GOOD TIME. And then when I got on the bus, our usual spot at the back was empty. I'd never felt so frantic in all my life.

At school, remembering what Caroline had said about Facebook, I walked by Tim's locker, expecting something to be written on it in big red letters. But it was clean. As I headed down the hall, I felt like everybody was staring at me with this kind of pitying smirk. Part of me wanted to scream, "I knew! This was not a shock to me! I knew!"

When I got to American history, Devon had stationed himself in the corner desk in the front row, right by the door. I was actually kind of glad there wouldn't be any way to avoid him, because what I wanted to do was look him right in the eye and see if there would be any sympathy or understanding or worry for his friend. I wanted to give him a chance to ask me how Tim was. So I kept my eyes on his as I walked toward the back, where Allie was already sitting. Devon drummed his pencil on the desk, looking around the room everywhere except at me.

So I stopped. And I said, real pointed, "Hey, Devon."

He caught the pencil short and finally looked up. "Oh. Hey, Wren."

His face looked just the slightest bit drawn, like he had to fake his usual friendliness. I thought what Caroline had said, about him not stopping Rachel from spreading the news all over the party. And my heart started beating with a fiery kind of anger.

"Devon," I said. "Don't you have anything you want to ask me?"

He tilted his head, and some color came back into his face. By now a couple of people around us were paying attention, and you could tell Devon was real aware of this. So he arranged his face in a way that seemed very deliberate. Like he thought my saying this was the funniest thing in the world. And he said, loud enough for pretty much everyone in the class to hear, "How's your gay boyfriend?"

There may have been a snicker or two, but I swear most of the room was quiet. Although I didn't raise my eyes, I had this sense of solidarity, like most everyone was on my—and more importantly Tim's—side. So I started to give up and head to the back of the room.

I heard Devon shuffle in his seat. I waited for him to say something else sarcastic and nasty. That's what I was braced for. Instead he started humming Og's song from the musical, "When I'm Not Near the Girl I Love." What an a-hole!

I heard him say then, "We should've known when we saw the tights."

Whoever he'd said it to not only laughed in this mean, disgusting way—wrecking that nice sense of solidarity I'd felt a moment before—but muttered the word "faggot." To which Devon said nothing at all, not a single word. And then he laughed too.

I swear I couldn't help it. Even though I knew better, what happened next felt like the only thing in the world to do. I turned around and walked over to Devon's desk and kicked him as hard as I could in the shin with my steel-toed cowboy boots.

"Ow," Devon said, in a tone that I will permit myself to notice was quite unmanly. "Are you crazy?"

As luck would have it, Ms. Durand chose that moment to walk into the classroom. "Wren," she said, clearly surprised. "*What* are you doing?"

"Kicking Devon," I said. And then, because obviously I was in trouble anyway, I lifted my foot and kicked him just as hard in the other shin.

*   *   *

In my whole life I had only been to the principal's office once, in first grade, when I stole a pack of Tic Tacs out of a substitute teacher's purse. Ms. Sincero, the principal at Cutty River, had made me call the substitute at home and apologize. I remember the phone call clearly. I called up the teacher and repeated everything Ms. Sincero whispered to me, about how I was sorry and I took personal responsibility. The sub forgave me, and then she said, "Is there anything else?"

"How are you doing?" I said, and she laughed. It made me happy, hearing that laugh, like what I'd done wasn't so bad and maybe she even still liked me a little bit.

But as I sat outside the principal's office at Williamsport High, I crossed my arms over my chest and narrowed my eyes in preparation for battle. Because no one in the world could make me apologize to Devon. I didn't care if they threatened to expel me. I was glad I'd kicked him, and I would do it again.

Which is exactly what I said to Mr. Bernacki when he finally called me into his office. "I'm glad I kicked him, and I'd do it again."

Mr. Bernacki looked up from the computer screen he'd been reading—probably my file. He pointed to the chair in front of his desk. "Have a seat, Ms. Piner."

I sat down. He gave me a little rigmarole about how

violence was never the correct course of action and wouldn't
be tolerated at Williamsport High School.

"That's all fine and well," I said. "But I'm not going to say
I'm sorry, because I'm not."

Ms. Sincero, my old principal, had been tall and young
and easy to make laugh. To me Mr. Bernacki looked about a
hundred years old, and like he hadn't found anything funny
since he was fifty. He sighed, took off his glasses to wipe
them clean, then propped them back on his nose.

"Ms. Piner."

"You can call me Wren."

"Yes, I'm aware that I can call you Wren. You, however,
seem entirely unaware of how to comport yourself in a principal's office."

I slumped in my chair while he lectured me, feeling like
even though Mr. Bernacki was so old and kind of mean, if
I told him the *reason* I'd kicked Devon, he'd be on my side.
But I just couldn't shake the feeling it wasn't my reason to
tell, because then what if he went ahead and told Tim's parents about it?

"Ms. Lang, my secretary, is on the phone with your parents now. You'll be excused from school for the rest of today
and tomorrow."

"You mean suspended?"

"This time we're going to call it excused. I am hoping
there won't be a next time."

"No, sir," I said.

"Please make sure to have all your assignments completed."

"Yes, sir."

He didn't say anything else, and after a few seconds of silence I realized it was time for me to go. I stood up, gave an awkward little good-bye wave, and let myself out of his office, hoping this would be my very last brush with any kind of law.

My dad came to get me in his Jeep. Up till now he had kept a low profile in terms of what had happened over the weekend. Yesterday all he'd said was that as long as I hadn't been drinking, none of it was any of his business, but he hoped I'd take note of what a mess my friends had gotten themselves into. As I climbed into the passenger seat he tried to look stern, but I could tell his heart wasn't in it.

"You want to tell me what happened, Wren?" he said, after he'd pulled the car away from the curb. "When they told me you'd kicked someone, I felt sure they had the wrong kid."

I told him about Devon, and how he'd acted. "But it wasn't just that one moment," I said. "I feel like ever since I met that guy he's been saying rude things about Tim without even knowing it. You know what I mean? If it weren't for people like him, saying mean things and not minding their own business, none of this would even be a problem. You know?"

"I sure do," Dad said. "I can certainly see how you would feel that way. And I agree, people like that, they sure do their share of making this world a tougher place to live."

I nodded, feeling tears pop into my eyes.

"But still," Dad said. "You can't kick them."

"Yes, sir," I said. Dad laughed, and I laughed along with him but only a little.

I guess Dad could tell how forlorn I felt, because out of the blue he offered to take me to the DMV for my driving test. He said it being a school day we could probably get in without an appointment. It took most of the morning, but by the end of it all I had a shiny North Carolina driver's license, even if my picture did look kind of sad. To celebrate, Dad took me to my favorite downtown restaurant called the Basics, which serves the best Southern food in the whole world. Even their spinach is delicious, and don't get me started on their biscuits. It wasn't exactly how you'd expect to be treated the afternoon you got "excused" for kicking a kid in American history, but I sure wasn't going to complain.

Soon as we got home I called Tim. He still wouldn't answer his phone, and I didn't think I could stand it another minute, not seeing him or even talking to him. I would have gone over to his house, but even though my parents weren't really mad, they said I couldn't leave the farm until it was time to go back to school. So I looked up his home phone on MSN White Pages.

"Hello?" Mr. Greenlaw said. It surprised me that he'd be at home in the middle of a Monday afternoon.

"Hello," I said. "May I please speak to Tim? This is Wren Piner."

There was a long pause on the other end, and I couldn't help but read a whole lot into it. While I waited for Mr. Greenlaw to say something, I suspected that he had found out Tim was gay and couldn't decide whether I was a part of the problem or a possible solution. I heard Mrs. Greenlaw's voice in the background, asking a question, and then I heard his father say my name.

"Just a minute, Wren," Mr. Greenlaw said.

I got up from the computer and walked upstairs to my room, then had to sit on my bed waiting for what seemed forever.

"Hi, Wren," Tim said. His voice sounded hollow and raspy, like he'd been crying. I couldn't imagine Tim crying. "I can't really talk now," he said.

There were a million things I wanted to ask him. One of those things—did his parents know—seemed to have been answered by this phone call. I had the weird sense that I was calling a home where a death had just occurred.

"Okay," I said. "I just wanted to check in and, you know, see if you were all right."

The silence on the other end told me what a stupid thing this was to say.

"Well," I said. "I just wanted to let you know that I think you're exactly right, exactly the way you are."

This wasn't the right thing to say either, because Tim started to cry. He cried in choked, deep sobs. I could only just make out him saying, "I'll call you later, Wren."

"Okay," I said into my phone, even though I knew there was nobody on the other end. I hung up and stared out the window. By now late afternoon had arrived, and the winter sunlight darkened over the east paddock. And for the first time that day I noticed something very strange: There were no horses there. Not a single one.

I ran to the windowsill and looked out. I had a good view of the entire paddock, and my eyes searched the treeless expanse as if a horse might magically appear. Never in my life had I seen it empty, except during hurricanes.

I took the steps three at a time, then lurched outside. Empty. In all the drama of the past few days with Tim and Allie and the party, I had not had a thought for one second about our farm and the horses. And now look what had happened. It felt like a bad dream, a terrible dream, the worst dream in the world.

By now I could hear my mother's voice calling to me. I

ran away from her, out toward the barn. I could hear her behind me, and my father, too. One of them might have said, "Don't worry, Wren," but that didn't help. I didn't trust them anymore. I truly believed they could have sold her, given her away—my horse, Pandora.

I slammed into the barn, my chest heaving. The familiar rustling from Pandora's stall greeted me, and she shuffled around and wound her neck out toward me the way she always did. I thought I might die from relief. As I ran to her, I saw we still had four horses left, including Sombrero. But at that moment Pandora was the only one I cared about. I slammed myself into her stall and wound my arms around her neck, burying my face in her dark-brown softness.

My mom and dad clattered into the barn, both of them out of breath. Now I got why they hadn't been mad about the thing with Devon.

"Now I get why you took me to get my license," I said, my voice muffled but fierce. "You needed to keep me away from the house while the horses were taken away."

I didn't look their way, just listened to the silence. Finally my mom said, "I'm sorry, Wren. We were going to talk to you about it tonight. I know I should have told you. It was just . . . it was so hard for me, honey." Her voice broke. "It was so hard for me to do, to let them go, and I knew that I couldn't hear any arguments against it. You know? I just had to bite the bullet and do it. I had to let it be done."

"Who took them?" I said.

"A rescue group. A national one. This woman came down from Kentucky, and she's going to distribute them to other rescues in different states."

Mom started rattling off which horses were going where in this weird, robotic voice, like she'd been going over and over it in her own head, trying to convince herself it would be all right. When she said that Sir Lancelot was going to a retirement center up north, I finally took my face away from Pandora and looked both my parents in the eye.

"Sir Lancelot isn't the only one who's going up north, is he?"

My parents shook their heads. I had this weird feeling, like I was the adult and they were the children.

"So it's true. We're moving to New Hampshire. It's a done deal."

They both started talking at once, their words running over each other, saying how it wouldn't be such a bad thing, how we would be living in a nice house on the campus, and we would take Daisy with us, and I would get this first-rate private-school education for free. Listening to them, I almost felt like my head would explode. Finally I screamed at them, at the top of my lungs, "Stop it!"

Pandora shied in her stall, and the other remaining horses pawed their hooves nervously. Mom and Dad just stood there, staring at me.

"Stop it," I whispered, ashamed of myself for scaring the horses. "Stop it and just go away."

"Wren . . . ," Mom said.

"Go away," I hissed, my teeth clenched, still regretful but fully prepared to yell again if I needed to.

The two of them shuffled out of the barn. I hated how defeated their footsteps sounded. Daisy stayed behind, her tags jingling nervously outside the stall. I let her in when I knew my parents were a good distance away. The two of us—Daisy and me—collapsed in a heap in the corner of Pandora's stall. We fell asleep and didn't wake up till it was dark outside, and my mother came back to bring me in for dinner.

"I don't want any dinner," I said. "Please leave me alone."

Mom didn't threaten or cajole or even plead with me. She just turned and walked away, those same sad footsteps. Daisy felt bad for her, I guess, because she scratched at the stall door until I gave up and let her out, and she ran to catch up with my mom. I sank back down onto the straw, wondering if anything would ever go right again.

It wasn't easy staying out in the barn, I will tell you that right now. Part of me wanted to give up and go have dinner, then climb the stairs to the comfort of my own bedroom. In the old days I would have found a way to get to Allie's house. Just a few days ago I would have gone to Tim's. But as things stood I didn't even have my phone with me, and I couldn't get any closer to running away than huddling in Pandora's stall. At least this way I'd know if someone came to get her.

I got a couple of old Indian blankets from Mom's office and hunkered down in the corner of Pandora's stall, wrapped up in the itchy wool and trying to imagine what my life in New Hampshire would be like. I bet they didn't have a drama program at that school, at least not as good as Williamsport High's. And how weird would it be to *live* with all the kids you went to school with? For example, I sure felt glad Devon and Rachel didn't live anywhere close to us right now. I closed my eyes and tried to let a picture form of what next year would hold, but it just seemed so foreign and odd, nothing would come into my head at all.

I must have dozed off again, because the next thing I knew I was sitting straight up in the dark, my heart pounding a million miles a minute. Something had woken me up. I knew that immediately, though it took me a few seconds to register where I was. Pandora's shuffling and snorting gave me a pretty good idea, and also let me know that whatever noise I'd heard hadn't been a dream. Somebody was in the barn, moving around. I could hear hands against the wall, the sound of someone making his way in the dark.

The light went on in my mom's office, casting a pale

shadow down the aisle of the barn. A few triangular slats of light made their way into the stall with Pandora and me. My heart slowed down a little. Probably it was just my mom, sneaking down to check on me. I felt a sudden flood of shame and guilt. Pulling one of the blankets over my shoulders, I got to my feet and headed toward the tack room.

The door had been left open, and something about the footsteps inside—heavy and furtive—made me pause. They didn't sound like my mom's. For one thing, whoever it was fumbled around like he didn't know where anything was. And also, it sounded like a man. I don't know how, it just did.

I flattened my back against the wall and sidled toward that open door. In my head a million thoughts raced, what I would do if there really was an intruder in there. *Daisy, you damn Hellhound, where are you and all your scary snarls when I need you?* I decided I would peek in, figure out who was there, and if the person looked sinister, I would bolt as fast as I could toward the house, screaming at the top of my lungs. Best plan I could come up with.

I heard the drawer open in my mom's desk, and then I heard the person cross the room and fiddle with keys. My whole body froze solid. Only one thing in there needed keys to open. Dad's gun case.

I decided not to bother peeking inside, just pushed off my heels and ran. But out of the corner of my eye I saw the person turn to see me sneak past in the shaft of light. A startled blond head. I skidded to a stop. Then I turned around and crossed the threshold of the office, where Tim stood, Dad's old Winchester clutched in his hands.

"Tim," I said, surprised at how clear and sharp my voice sounded after all the sleep and fear. "What the hell do you think you're doing?"

He blinked at me. Never in my life had I wished so badly for a moment to turn out to be a dream. I didn't know what to do. I knew I needed to get that gun away from him, but I didn't know how. It was so scary and so surreal. Tim, except for the rifle, looked perfect. He had on blue jeans and a flannel shirt under a big raglan sweater, and his hair looked mussed but the way a Hollywood stylist might muss it to make him look even cuter. He looked like the world's most perfect broad-shouldered, sun-streaked, all-American boyfriend.

"You're the only one I know who has guns," he said simply.

"Tim," I said, my stomach clutching up. "Please. There's nothing in the world you need a gun for."

He stood there, thinking on this. He looked down at the rifle. It looked weirdly natural in his hands. I didn't think it was loaded, but on the other hand, Dad wasn't always as careful as he should be about things like that. Thankfully, at that moment Tim had it pointed at the outside wall. If he pointed it in the opposite direction and it went off accidentally, it might go through the panels and hit one of our last remaining horses.

"My parents know," he said.

"I could tell," I said, "when I called."

"Do you know what they're fixing to do? Send me away to this place where you learn how not to be gay." He said this and then just stood there, looking hopeless.

"How can you learn not to be gay?" I said.

Tim just shook his head. Reaching out my hands for the rifle, I stepped toward him. He backed away, clutching it to his chest.

"You don't even know how to use that," I said.

"Don't have to aim," he said. "Just put it in my mouth and pull the trigger."

My spine turned to ice. "Tim," I whispered. "This is one moment. One single second in time. Please don't do this. If you can just wait for this moment to pass, things will get better. I know they will."

He snorted, like this was the stupidest thing he'd ever heard. I took another step toward him. It might have been my imagination, but he seemed to relax his grip on the gun. So I took another step.

"Think of the play," I said. "Think of singing, and acting, and throwing a ball around, and everything you love. Think of me," I said, my voice rising with desperation. "You don't want to die, Tim."

"But that's the thing," he said. "I do. I would rather die than have to live like this the rest of my life. None of that other stuff even matters. It sucks so bad, Wren. I can't even tell you, I can't even describe it. I hate myself and I hate my life, and I can't change anything. I don't want to change, and I don't want to stay this way. I can't think of anything else to do but die."

All the while he spoke, he lowered the gun bit by bit, and his grip loosened. Before I had a chance to think about it, I took one huge step toward him and grabbed the gun. I ripped it out of Tim's hands, and he reached out and tugged back, and guess what? It went off, with such a sharp retort that we both went flying, tumbling into the bales of hay stacked against the wall. The rifle skittered across the floor and landed in a corner, leaving me and Tim on the other side of the room, his weight pinning me to the ground. He looked at me for a second with an expression I never could have imagined on him, this look of pure rage. Then he grabbed my head in his hands and kissed me, hard, on the mouth. He kissed me with his eyes closed, and his lips open a little, exactly the way I'd wanted him to kiss me that first day back in the fall.

And I kissed him back. I kissed him back with all my might. I put all the love I had for him into that kiss, all the longing, all the wanting. Maybe they wouldn't have to send him away to some un-gaying camp. Maybe I could do it for them, for him, for everybody.

Tim pulled away from me but still kept his hands on my face. He stared straight at me, looking a little bit more like the boy I knew. Something in his expression had softened, though when he spoke his voice sounded fierce.

"Wren," he said, "I love you too much to love you. Do you understand what I'm saying? Do you understand what I mean?"

I nodded. And I didn't say it, but hoped he knew, that I also loved him too much—no matter how I wanted—to ask him to be something that he simply never could.

The gunshot woke my parents. Lights were turned on, and robes grabbed; frantic footsteps along with a jangling and ferociously barking dog made their way across the lawn that wouldn't be ours much longer, to the barn that was on its way to being emptied of horses. My parents found me and Tim there, kneeling on the floor, clinging to each other, both of us sobbing as if the world had ended, which—in its own way, for both of us—it certainly had.

Sixteen

I remember that night in a lot of different ways: some sad, some less sad. For example, I can't help but feel that's when my mom got her spirit back. She was the one who ran and flung her arms around Tim and me, weeping with happiness to find us both alive, while my dad emptied the Winchester and then checked every other rifle in the case before locking it and stuffing the key in his pocket. I knew in that moment none of those rifles would be coming north with us.

We all made our way back to the kitchen. Mom put the teakettle on to boil, and Dad poured himself a shot of whiskey. He started right in, insisting we call Tim's parents. Mom kept shushing him, then coaxed the whole story out of Tim. He sat there at our table and told her everything, as opposed to the bits and pieces he'd told me.

"We kept getting all these crank calls," Tim said. "I

couldn't see how my parents wouldn't figure it out. And I just couldn't go back to school today. So I told them."

Tim's father had thrown up. He turned white as a ghost, excused himself from the room, and left Tim and Mrs. Greenlaw in the living room, listening to him retch away in the half bath. "I just sat there," Tim said, "thinking that I make my own father sick."

When that part was over his mother cried, and his father yelled, and they got their pastor on the phone and he came right over with all sorts of literature about where they could send him to cure him of his sinful inclinations. While Tim told us all this he was trying to drink his tea, but his hands were shaking too hard and he kept having to put it back down. As my mom listened, I could see some sort of force lifting her up from the center of her being. Suddenly she didn't look defeated anymore. She looked energized, and I knew exactly what was happening. She'd found someone new to rescue—someone who didn't require acres of land and regular veterinary care.

"Don't you worry, Tim," she said. "I'm going to talk to your parents. You can stay right here with us until they see this thing clearly."

"Elizabeth," Dad said. His eyes had gone wide, and I could see him battling not to roll them.

Mom held up her hand like a crossing guard stopping traffic. "Let me tell you something, honey," she said, keeping her eyes on Tim. "You don't need to go anywhere. You don't need to get changed. You are exactly as God made you, and you are perfect. Do you understand that?"

She reached out across the table and took both Tim's hands in hers, stopping their shaking. "You see?" she said. "Ten fingers. I'm guessing you have ten toes, too?"

Tim smiled a little with the corners of his mouth and bloodshot eyes, and then he nodded.

"Well, then," Mom said. "No adjustments needed. Why don't you just get some rest and try not to worry about anything else tonight. Okay?"

Now it was my turn to roll my eyes. I loved the way Mom kept instructing people not to worry. If only it were that easy!

She sent Dad to get something of his for Tim to sleep in. We all went upstairs, and when Dad handed Tim a pair of striped pajamas—his newest, nicest ones—Tim said thank you. And then he said, "Mr. and Mrs. Piner, I feel weird asking this. But would y'all mind if I slept in Wren's bedroom? I just really don't think I can handle being alone right now."

Well. If you want a long moment of awkward silence, that is one way to go about getting it. I could see Dad's face, a tightness around his jaw, like for a split second he wondered if this whole thing was all some elaborate ploy. Part of me wanted to make a joke about how they could be confident my honor would stay secure, given the situation. But the bigger part of me knew I wouldn't be making any jokes that had to do with a person's sexuality, not anytime soon, and hopefully not ever.

Finally Mom put her hand on Tim's shoulder. "That's fine with us, honey," she said. "You just make sure to get some sleep. Okay?"

Tim nodded. While he used the bathroom, I changed into my own pajamas and did my best to get the straw out of my hair. Tim changed in my room while I brushed my teeth. The one thing I didn't bother with was pulling the twin mattress out from under my bed. Tim and I crawled into bed together, my head resting on his chest and his arms tight around me. Despite everything, it felt powerfully nice to sleep being held this way; not only because I felt safe, and protected, and loved, but because I could feel from his arms that Tim was strong enough to get through whatever hardship the days and years ahead might hold.

It occurs to me that I never told you what I decided to write about for my history of Williamsport paper. The topic I ended up choosing was the first interracial marriage to legally take place in the city, Nathan and Ophelia Brookwood. Nathan was white, and Ophelia was African American. They got married in 1968. Ophelia had just died last year, but I got to talk to her granddaughter on the phone. Researching this paper I learned all kinds of things, like the fact that Ohio was the first state to make it legal for people of different races to marry, and that was in 1887. The next state to allow it was Oregon, but that wasn't until 1951! And by different races I don't just mean black and white people marrying each other, but Asian, and Native American, and just about any color you can think of. None of it was allowed. The truth is that until 1967 only fifteen states didn't consider miscegenation—a fancy/ugly word for interracial marriage—an out-and-out crime. Then this couple from Virginia whose last name was Loving (I'm not kidding, their real names were Mildred and Richard Loving) got married legally in Washington, DC, then got arrested in Virginia, where they lived. The police burst in on them in their own bedroom! Well, thank goodness there was some outrage over this, and the case made it all the way to the Supreme Court, where it was decided that banning inter-racial marriage was unconstitutional. So in 1967, the other thirty-five states, including North Carolina, had to take those miscegenation laws off the books. Hip hip hooray.

The reason I tell you this now is that the second day of my suspension I worked on my paper while Mom and Tim went for a long walk. Sitting at my laptop in the kitchen (my parents didn't allow me to go online upstairs), I dou-ble-checked my research and put the finishing touches on everything I had to say. I included a little personal history about how Holly and James were getting married and how happy I felt about it, and at the same time how sick to my stomach it made me that such a thing would ever have been considered a crime. I also wrote about how things had certainly changed since 1967. Even though an old woman in the grocery store once told Holly she should be ashamed of herself, most days she and James can hold hands on the street in Raleigh or anywhere else, with nobody minding a single bit, or hardly even noticing.

Reading over what I'd written so far, I worried I was making the world today sound a little too rosy. So I added some stories James had told me about patients who refused to let him treat them, even when they were screaming from pain. And I put in a paragraph about how J. K. Polk High, which is 76 percent African American, has much fewer resources than Williamsport High, which is 83 percent white.

But mostly I wanted my paper to focus on the positive stuff. For people of different races who fell in love with each other, forty-four years—a little bit longer than either of my parents had been alive—was the space of time between police bursting into bedrooms and just perfectly normal. I wondered if a similar space of time waited for Tim, and it would take forty-four years before a pair of guys could kiss at a party without causing a gigantic fuss. It seemed to me that was a long time to wait for the world to recognize its own mean silliness. After all, back when the Lovings got married, most people in the world probably didn't care one way or another. Most people were just going about their own lives, thinking on their own problems—paying the electric bill, saving the family farm—and not minding a bit who married who. They finally stood up, though, when the Lovings got burst in on in their very own bedroom. That's when the whole world sat up and took notice. Hey, the world said. They aren't doing harm to anybody. So how about letting them be?

When Mom and Tim got back from their walk, Mom called Tim's parents to let them know he was with us. She happened to get his father, and from where Tim and I sat at the kitchen table we could hear him shout through the receiver about how Tim could just stay away until he decided to do what was right and fix himself. Mom was shaking by the time she hung up. Tim looked awful shaky himself, but not near so desperate as he did last night. I think he was relieved to be over here with us.

"Well," Mom said later, at dinner. She passed around a bowl of green beans. "Wren's got to go back to school tomorrow. What do you think, Tim? What are you going to do?"

Tim took a heaping pile of green beans, then passed the bowl to me. He moved his food around on his plate with his fork, though none of us had started eating yet. "I think I'll go too, Mrs. Piner," he said. "I think I'm tired of being kept away from my own damn life."

"Good man," Dad said. My parents smiled at him, but inside I felt this coldness. I thought of everything the Lovings had to go through before things finally got put right, and even though I admired them for it, it was nothing I would ever wish on anyone I loved.

The next morning Dad said we could take his Jeep to school, but Tim said no. "I'm guessing I'll have to get used to staring," he said. "I might as well get my practice on the bus."

We waited together at the end of my driveway, holding hands. I felt glad that we only had a week and a half before winter vacation, so no matter how bad things ended up being, Tim wouldn't have to bear it for long. Or at least he'd get a break from it very quickly. We watched as the bus came rumbling down the road.

"I wonder if Jay's gone back to school," Tim said. It was the first time I'd heard him say Jay's name since before all this happened.

"I didn't see him on Monday," I said. "But then I wasn't there very long." Tim smiled a little, and I hoped it was because he was picturing me kicking Devon.

The bus wheezed to a stop, and the door opened. "Well," Tim said, with a deep intake of breath. "Here goes nothing."

I stepped onto the bus first, and Tim followed. And you know what? Nothing happened. All the kids, they just sat in their seats, continuing their conversations. One or two might have looked over at us like they had heard about it, but they mostly just looked kind of curious. I saw one girl smile at Tim, like she wanted to make sure he knew he was welcome.

The two of us filed down the aisle to our usual seat in back and flopped down, panting like we'd just sprinted through the first leg of a series of trials. All I could do now was hope that once Tim got to school, whatever mean and bigoted people there were would find a way to mind their manners, not to mention their own damn business.

They never do, though, do they? All morning Tim and I stuck close, even though we didn't have any classes together. First we got off the bus, our arms kind of pressing against each other. He came with me to my locker, then we went to his, and I walked him to his first class. It seemed kind of weird that I would be protecting him when I barely came up to his shoulder, but that's what it felt like. Tim tried his best to look calm, but I could tell by his face he felt anything but.

I got to every class late that morning on account of my resolve to walk with Tim to every one of his, and that included American history, which worked out just fine because when I arrived Ms. Durand was already there, which meant Devon couldn't say a word to me. Luckily, he had positioned himself on the other side of the classroom anyway, so I didn't even have to look his way as I headed to the back to sit next to Allie. She waved at me and mouthed, "How's Tim?"

I shrugged. How could I even begin to answer that?

As Ms. Durand talked on and on about the post–Civil War economy in the South, Allie passed me a note. It said, *Jay came back yesterday, and they wouldn't let him in the locker room.*

Who? I wrote back. *The football team?*

She nodded. I wrote, *Why didn't you text me or something?*

Allie looked over at Ms. Durand, who had turned to write something on the board. Then she handed the paper back to me. *Can't text. Cell phone confiscated. Plus, I didn't want to freak you out. But maybe you guys should avoid the cafeteria.*

Caroline Jones was of the same opinion. When I went to collect Tim from calculus, she stood there with him in the hall. "They really busted up Jay's face," she told us, adding that the main two kids who'd done it had been suspended and might even be expelled. "But the rest of the football team is super pissed that you guys were in the locker room with them all those times," Caroline said.

"Maybe I should tell them it wasn't all that exciting," Tim said.

Caroline bit her lip. "Nobody thought you'd come back," she said. "But I'm betting by now people will for sure be watching out for you in the cafeteria. So we should go somewhere else."

We hardly ever ate in the cafeteria anyway, so this didn't

seem like such a radical suggestion. I said, "Let's eat outside on the bleachers. It's not that cold."

"I'll go with you," Caroline said.

Tim headed for his locker, fast. Caroline and I found ourselves trotting to keep up with him. As we passed, lots of heads turned our way. Hardly anyone said a word, and I thought we'd made it, when one kid hissed, "Homo." And then another threw a crumpled-up piece of paper at him.

Even so, I thought—not so bad. Out of about a hundred kids crowding these hallways, two of them cared enough to be mean. Then I thought, what if the other ninety-eight stepped up and did something about that?

Tim opened his locker and traded his books for his lunch. He turned to me and Caroline.

"Listen," he said. "If they want to kick my ass, they're going to do it, right? I might as well get this over with."

Caroline and I looked at each other. "Well," she said, nodding. "I guess maybe it's safer to eat in the cafeteria anyway. There's not much they can do with teachers around."

So we all took deep breaths and walked in together, automatically looking at the table where Devon and Rachel and a bunch of their cronies sat eating. It may have been my imagination, but the buzz of the room seemed to lower the second we walked in. I could see Rachel elbow Devon, who looked right over at us. Another thing that might have been my imagination: Devon looked kind of sad, maybe even worried, as his eyes settled on Tim.

I could see Allie, sitting with Ginny and Jesse at a table in the corner. She waved us over. Tim looked in that direction, then started heading toward Devon and Rachel's table. Caroline grabbed his shirt before I had a chance.

"Whoa there, cowboy," she said. "Let's not take this too far, okay?"

Tim stopped for a moment, then gave in and let us pull him over to Allie's table. We sat down, all of us still sort of looking around to see if things had died down.

"So," Jesse said to Tim. "How's your first day out of the closet?"

"Harrowing," Tim said, and we all laughed a little. Tim sipped from his water bottle but didn't look ready to eat the lunch my mother had packed for him, which I noticed had a lot more food than mine. She apparently thought feeding a boy would be similar to feeding a grizzly bear.

After a few minutes of awkward silence, it seemed to me things got a little normal. The chatter in the cafeteria went back to its usual decibel. Jesse told us he liked the play, and Ginny made a joke about Allie at the cast party. Allie rolled her eyes, then said to everyone, though I had a feeling it was especially to me, "But guess what?"

"What?" I said.

"As anyone could have predicted, I am grounded for two whole weeks. Have to go home directly after school, no going out on weekends, double chore load, etc. etc. But when my parents sat me down to give me my punishment, they also said they'd been talking about their reaction to the whole modeling thing, and they decided they'd been unfair. So after Christmas they're going to let me sign up with the local agency and just see what happens. Just local stuff, to see if I like it and if I get hired."

I looked at her from across the table. For the first time I noticed she wasn't wearing any makeup, her hair was long and loose, her eyes were huge. She looked like her old self, and I thought anybody would be nuts not to see she was meant to be a model.

"And something else," she said. "I'm going back to Cutty River School."

"Next year?" I said, not bothering to mask the surprise in my voice.

"No," Allie said, glancing around the table for maximum dramatic effect. "After winter break."

We all stared at her. Ginny looked like she might start crying. "Maybe I can go back too," she said, in a small voice.

Allie smiled at her and said, "That'd be great. We could carpool. My parents are none too happy about making that drive. The whole reason they moved to Williamsport was so they wouldn't have to!"

"Well," I said. "It's only for a couple years, anyway."

"Six months," Allie corrected me. "Then I'll have my license and I can drive myself."

Her parents were slightly less maniacal about things like that. Still, it hit me what I'd said before. High school was just only for this short period of time. I looked over at Tim and I could tell he was thinking the same thing, and that maybe it comforted him a little bit.

Unfortunately, we didn't get a chance to discuss this, or even ask Allie more questions about going back to Cutty River School, because out of nowhere three football players were standing around our table.

"Hey, Greenlaw," one of them said to Tim. "I see you're hanging out with faggots now."

Jesse slumped down in his chair a little. Tim looked up.

"Yeah," Tim said. "I guess I finally figured out where I belong."

"Too bad it took you so long."

Tim shrugged. I could tell he couldn't think of anything to say, but I felt so proud of him, how brave he looked, sitting there, staring up at his old friends. I looked across the room to where Devon just sat, watching.

One of the guys shoved Tim's shoulder. His chair tilted a little. "Don't you have anything to say, faggot?"

I stood up and said, "Hey. Why don't you just leave him alone?"

Allie stood up too, right beside me, so she was practically

eye to eye with the guy who'd shoved Tim. "Why is it any of your business anyway?" she said.

I guess because he couldn't think of a reply, the guy grabbed Tim by the collar and pulled him out of his chair. Tim was just as big as he was but didn't fight back as the guy pressed him against the wall.

"You know," the football player said to Tim, "I was pretty pissed when you ditched us to be a little leprechaun. But that doesn't compare to how I felt when I found out what you really are."

At that moment, despite his size, Tim suddenly looked smaller—vulnerable. Really vulnerable. "Hey," I said again. My voice didn't come out at all like I wanted it to, more pleading than confrontational. "Leave him the hell alone!" I tried pulling at the guy's arm, but he shrugged me off like I was no more than a pesky fly. In that motion I could feel how strong he was, and how mad. My heart pounded away, and I waited for a teacher to step in, but so far all a couple of them had done was step closer, waiting to see how things would play out.

Luckily, one person in the cafeteria was a little braver— and a lot bigger—than this. He flew across the cafeteria in such a blur that I hardly recognized him until he'd grabbed the guy who had hold of Tim and threw him on the ground. The guy kind of half lay there, clearly surprised, looking up at the other football player who'd sat out that season: Tyler.

"You about done here?" Tyler said. When one of the other guys started to answer, Tyler interrupted him and said even louder, "YOU ABOUT DONE HERE?"

The guy pulled himself off the floor and brushed himself off, even though he didn't look as if he'd gotten very dirty. Then the three of them walked off. Tyler clapped Tim on the shoulder and said, "You doing all right, Og?"

"Yeah," Tim said. "I'm doing all right. Thanks." He kind of raised one shoulder and then the other, like making sure everything still worked. Then he sat back down, and Tyler took the seat next to him. We all kind of stared at one another for a minute, and then all the kids at the other tables went back to eating and talking. Everyone at our table—Tyler, Allie, Jesse, Ginny, Caroline, and me—sat there, just kind of shell-shocked.

And for a moment I had this fantasy: that I would climb up onto our table and yell out to the whole cafeteria: *How many of you care that Tim is gay? Raise your hands!* And there would be this tiny smattering of raised hands. Then I would say, *How many people couldn't care less if Tim is gay?* And then almost everyone would raise a hand, and some people would even cheer, and everyone would start clapping.

But I couldn't bring myself to actually do it, even though I am an extroverted and outspoken person who never minds a spotlight. Instead I just sat there, staring across the table at Tim, glad that a bodyguard had turned up and wishing there were something more I could have done to help.

On the bus ride home Tim started talking about baseball. With everything going on, you'd think that might be the last thing on his mind. But he was so bummed about it. "What sucks is knowing I can't play ball again," he said. "I love it so much. Especially football. It kind of breaks my heart that I can't ever play again."

"Maybe you could," I said, though I knew my voice sounded doubtful. I couldn't help thinking of Jay. That big huge guy! Not safe in the locker room.

"No way," Tim said. "Not worth it. No matter how much I want to, it's not worth it. Tyler can't watch out for me round the clock. Hell" —he put his hand up to shade his eyes, like he was blocking the sun—"maybe he'd feel different too if I were in the locker room with him."

"Well," I said, trying to think of something comforting, "you can still be in plays. There's no locker room there."

"And my parents think God hates me," Tim went on, as if I hadn't said anything. He turned and looked out the window. Whatever tears he'd been battling had gone away, but he looked so wiped out. I couldn't stand to think he had to wake up and do it all over again, again, and again, every day, not to mention figure out what he was going to do about his parents. He couldn't stay at our house forever, after all. Even we couldn't do that.

Then I had a thought. A good thought. "God couldn't hate you too much," I told him. "He sure made you good at everything. Plus, you know. Kind of gorgeous?"

Tim gave me a small smile. And I thought, here we are, our cover blown. And Tim probably knowing, at least a little bit, how I'd felt the whole time. But still we sat right next to each other, close as could be. Best friends. That's what I'd be left with after everything was said and done. And I thought that as long as I could see him, safe and well and surviving, that would be just fine with me.

As if he could read my thoughts, Tim reached out and took my hand, his fingers drumming lightly against all that scar tissue on my palm, just some of the remnants of this fall that would stay with me forever.

Seventeen

That night after dinner, when Tim had gone upstairs to do some homework, my parents called me into the living room. "We haven't really had a chance to fill you in on what's going to happen," Mom said carefully. "What with everything that's been going on."

I sat in the middle of the couch. The two of them each sat in an armchair, facing me, but a little ways away from each other so I had to keep turning my head from one to the other as they tried to explain. The bank hadn't approved the sale yet, but they expected it would. They were hoping to stay in the house till the end of June; the buyers were sympathetic, they said, so they didn't think it would be a problem. Then when I finished tenth grade, we'd be moving to New Hampshire. We were going to live at the Hillsdale School in one half of a big house. The other half was a dorm where a bunch of girls lived. I would go to Hillsdale—a really, *really*, good school! they said about a million times—as a student free of charge.

"Are there guys there too?" I asked.

"Yes," Dad said, sounding disappointed. "It's coed."

"Do they put on plays?"

Mom said that she'd looked into it, and they did, and that the drama program was strong. I could even take drama as an elective class for credit. That sounded not so bad, I let myself think. While she ran the riding program, Dad would look for work, hopefully with the US Forest Service, but also at colleges. "It's not too far from Boston," Dad said. "There are lots of possibilities."

I sat there quietly. Every word spelled out the end of life as I'd always known it. At this point, though, there wouldn't be much good in screaming about it. My parents hadn't created this situation on purpose. They'd done their best, and were still doing their best: to make things right, and to take care of me as best they could. So I just sat there, listening to them, these two people who had always loved me no matter what. Who always would love me no matter what. That last part used to feel like a matter of course, and nothing to be grateful for. Needless to say, I now knew the reverse was true.

"And, honey," Mom said, her voice suddenly sounding fake bright. "Part of the deal we worked out includes the board of one horse. We can take one horse with us. And I've decided that's going to be Pandora."

I felt my heart give a leap—I got to keep Pandora! Then, just as quickly, it sank like a stone, as I realized that keeping Pandora meant not keeping Sombrero. Tears filled up my eyes. I couldn't believe Mom would give up Sombrero, and from the look on her face, neither could she. She rubbed her hands across her knees, like now that she'd said it there was no turning back, and she needed to comfort herself.

"Mom," I started. I didn't want to say what had come into my head. The thought that she'd agree terrified me. At the same time, I knew that she *should* agree. After all these years, after everything she'd done for these horses, the one we kept should be her favorite. Not mine.

So I knew what I had to do. Take a deep breath. Gather up every little bit of courage I had, and say it as fast as possible, before I had a chance to change my mind.

"Mom," I said. "I think the horse we take along with us should be yours. It should be Sombrero. I really think that."

By the last word my voice had started catching, so "that" almost sounded like a little sob. Mom's mouth twitched a little at the corner. I could see her resist looking over at Dad, who had shifted a little, recrossing his legs and taking off his glasses.

"I'm proud of you for saying so," Mom said. "But my decision is final. It's Pandora we're taking with us."

Probably a better person—a more grown-up person—would have argued the point a little longer. But I must admit that relief and sadness washed over me at the very same time. I got off the couch and threw my arms around her. "Thank you, Mom," I said. "Thank you."

Since that first very bad night, Tim had slept in the guest room. Now I went upstairs and knocked on the door. He wasn't doing homework, just sitting on the bed, staring out the window with his phone in his hands. I plunked down next to him.

"I called Jay," he said. "His parents are going to home-school him for the rest of the year. They wanted to press charges against the guys who beat him up, but he talked them out of it."

"Maybe he could go to Cutty River," I said.

"His parents are going to try to get him into Ezra Lion." Ezra Lion was this program they had at the college, where you could go to high school and your first two years of college at the same time. Mostly geniuses and social misfits ended up there.

"You could go to Ezra Lion too," I said.

"Not without my parents enrolling me," Tim said. "At least I don't think I can. And I'm already giving up sports. Am I supposed to give up drama, too?" Ezra Lion didn't have extracurricular activities.

We sat there a minute, and then his phone buzzed. Tim looked at it. "My mom," he said. "She keeps calling, but she doesn't leave any message."

"Why don't you pick up?" I suggested gently.

He shrugged, miserable. From downstairs, the doorbell rang. I could hear my dad answer the door, and then he called up to us. "Tim! Someone's here to see you."

"Go on down," Tim whispered. "See who it is."

I had only seen her once before, in the auditorium after *Finian's Rainbow*, when there hadn't been time to properly introduce us. But as I walked down the stairs it only took a second to recognize the girl standing in our front hall. She had long, thick blond hair, and freckles, and pretty blue eyes just like Tim's.

"Hey," I said, sounding real glad to see her.

"Hey," she said back. "You must be Wren. I'm Kathy Greenlaw. Tim's sister."

By now you might be thinking that Tim's parents were the most coldhearted people on the planet. That's sure what I thought. I knew, for example, that my mom had called and told them that we found Tim in our barn with a gun to his head. And still they hadn't come to collect him and tell him everything would be all right. After three whole days! They let their only son go and face the idiots at school with no support from his family. I couldn't imagine how anybody could think that kissing another boy was a sin but it was perfectly okay to just abandon your own child in his time of deepest need.

Luckily, Kathy came to give us behind-the-scenes information. "I came home from school as soon as I could," she said. She, my parents, Tim, and I all sat around the kitchen table. Kathy sat next to Tim; she'd pulled her chair up real close to him.

"Tim," she said, "I want to bring you home."

Tim shook his head vehemently.

"There's not going to be any antigay therapy," Kathy said. "I promise you right now."

"I don't believe that," Tim argued. "They're just saying that to get me to come home. Then Pastor Lee's going to be there ready to haul me away." He glared at his sister. "Kathy, I don't want to be prayed over. I don't want to be changed. I just want to be me."

Kathy nodded. "I'm on the same page, Tim. Listen. I made an appointment with a different Lutheran minister, for you and me, tomorrow. His church isn't breaking with the main church. They don't mind gay pastors. They don't mind gay people."

"Is the pastor gay?" Tim said, right away.

"No," Kathy said. "But he's really open-minded." She said that she and Tim could talk to this man together, and maybe he would come up with ideas for talking to his parents. "Mom and Dad are upset," Kathy said, "but they love you, and they've got to see it's better to switch churches than children."

Tim nodded, but he didn't look especially convinced. In

the end I think he agreed to go talk to the pastor so he'd have an excuse not to go to school tomorrow. And I sure couldn't blame him for that.

Next morning before first bell, Allie was waiting for me by my locker. "Where's Tim?" she said.

"He's with his sister."

"Oh," she said. "Is his family taking him out of school? I heard Jay's not coming back."

"I don't think they know yet," I said. It really wasn't my business to tell her what jerks Tim's parents were being, so I didn't get into it any more than that. Allie leaned against the locker next to mine while I dug out my books. I said, "I'm sorry I didn't call to talk more about Cutty River."

"I'm not allowed to talk on the phone anyway," she said, looking a little dejected, like she thought this was the reason I hadn't called her.

"Sorry," I said, wondering if we'd ever be able to have a conversation without both of us apologizing a hundred times. "It's been pretty intense at my house. But I have to know! How'd you get your parents to let you switch schools?"

"It was a lot easier than I thought," Allie said. "They think I haven't been myself since I started coming here. And they're so happy that there won't be any cheerleading in my future. Jesse's going back too, because his parents are scared after what happened with Jay. Ginny's parents won't let her switch midyear. But I bet yours would let you go next year if you wanted. But you probably don't want to. I mean, you seem pretty happy here."

She said that last part gently, no sarcasm or meanness at all. I slammed my locker door shut and took a deep breath. "I'm not going here or to Cutty River," I said. "I'm going to prep school in New Hampshire." This sounded so ridiculous, still, that I couldn't help laughing a little. Allie just stood there, staring at me. When she realized I wasn't kidding, she put her hand over her mouth. I told her about the farm being sold, and my mom's new job.

"At least you get to bring Pandora," she said. We started walking down the hall together.

"Yeah," I said, trying not to think about everything else, everything I'd have to leave behind.

"You'll need to buy a lot of warm clothes," Allie said. I hadn't thought about that, but she was right. I felt a moment of panic, like where would we get the money, but then I figured that even up north it would take a couple of months to get seriously cold. By then my mother would have gotten a paycheck or two, so maybe we'd have enough money for a few pairs of snow boots.

"I guess we'll have the whole fall to figure all that out," I said to Allie. She nodded. By now we were standing outside the door to my first-period class.

"Well," she said. "I'll see you at lunch?"

I nodded and waved to her, then stood for a minute and watched her long, dark ponytail swish down the hall, trying to figure out if I would miss her when we left, or if I had missed her so long that by now I was over it.

That afternoon I rode the bus home by myself. In my usual seat at the back, I pulled my phone out of my bag and looked for the umpteenth time to see if Tim had checked in. Nada. I wondered how the meeting with the pastor had gone, how his reunion with his family was going. Part of me felt scared that his sister had shown up as a double agent and by now Tim was halfway to an antigay boot camp. What the heck did they do at those places, anyway? And what woman would want to marry a man who had to use all his spiritual energy not to be gay?

Me, I had to remind myself. *I am one of those women.*

When I got home, my mom was on her knees on the kitchen floor, digging through a cupboard full of pots and pans. She looked up at me and sighed. "I can't figure out what I can't bear to part with," she said.

I gave a little snort, and she hauled herself off the floor to sit down at the table with me. "I know," she said. "This whole year is turning out to be a lesson in what we can and can't bear to part with."

"Mom," I said, "you've got six months. You know? Why not give it a rest for a while?"

"You're right," she said. "I'm sorry." She closed the cupboard door like that was the end of it, but I knew as soon as I was out of sight she'd be back at it again. My mother needs her projects. I asked her if she would read my paper for American history. It was pretty much finished, but seeing as it was due tomorrow, it wouldn't hurt to have her check it over for grammar and all that. While she read it, I texted Tim. After a few minutes of waiting for a return message to chime, I went outside and sat on the porch swing. It was colder than I expected, and I wished I'd put my jacket on, but I didn't go back inside.

Lately I had been trying not to look at our farm as if it were the last time I'd ever see it; but just now I was feeling melancholy anyway, so I really let my eyes roam around the view. Pandora and Sombrero and the other two horses grazed on the hill. There were so many longleaf pines that even though the grass had started to brown, the main impression I had staring out was of green. From where I sat I couldn't see the water in the river through the overhang of moss and vines, but I knew it ran low even for this time of year. I wondered if that alligator would make its way back here this summer. Chances are we would never know.

Mom came outside, my paper in her hand. I could see red pen where she'd marked mistakes. She sat next to me and slid it into my lap. "It's good, Wren," she said. "Really good. You should send a copy to Holly."

"She probably knows all that stuff already," I said.

"Still. She'll be touched you're thinking about it."

I nodded. Then I said, "I don't see why it takes so long for people to figure out what's obvious. I mean, isn't it funny how Holly and James getting married seems perfectly normal? When less than fifty years ago it wouldn't even have been legal in most of the country."

Mom tilted her head. She looked out in the direction of the river, and I wondered if she was thinking about the alligator too. "I always think," she said, "that the world is like a child. It's still growing up and learning what's right. Like when you're two, and you throw temper tantrums and snatch toys out of other kids' hands. Or when you're six, and you only like girls and hate guys. But then you get a little older, and you learn life is easier if you behave better, more kindly. The world is maturing just like a person. It takes time to learn what's right and wrong. Maybe one day it will grow out of prejudice and meanness. It's done some good work in that direction. But it's sure not there yet."

"It's taking pretty stinking tiny little baby steps," I said.

"Gay marriage is legal in more and more states now," Mom said, though I hadn't mentioned anything about Tim, or gay marriage, not aloud or in my paper.

"But not all of them," I said.

"More than there used to be. And you know one of those states? New Hampshire."

I laughed. "Maybe we should bring Tim with us," I said. "Not that he wants to get married anytime soon. I hope."

"I'm sure he wants to stay with his family," Mom said, and I looked at her like she'd gone crazy. "Listen," she said. "They love him. They're wrongheaded right now, but I know they'll come around."

"You didn't need to come around," I said. "You accepted him right away."

"I was never taught differently," Mom said. "My parents made sure I knew what was right. Just like we did with you."

I had never thought of it that way. "We're lucky," I said. A few moments ago, surveying our soon-to-be-lost homestead, I would not have used that phrase to describe our family.

Mom laughed. "I'm glad you think so," she said. "Now go upstairs and clean up this paper." She gave me a light shove, just enough to slide me off the swing, and I headed upstairs to get to work.

Eighteen

Holly and James got married on the last day of May in a sunset ceremony at Wilbur Beach. I was maid of honor, and kind of best man, too, because they didn't have anyone stand up with them except for me. They said they chose me because if I hadn't fallen into that fire, they might never have come back together. Standing in the orange glow reflecting off the ocean, watching the two of them hold hands and recite their vows, I felt pretty sure they would have gotten back together one way or another no matter what. Some things are just meant to be.

I have never been one to turn down credit, never mind whether I deserve it or not. But if you ask me, one reason they didn't have a real best man—my dad, for example—was that there wouldn't have been enough people left to watch the ceremony. The only other people there were my parents, James's sister and mother, two friends from the hospital, and the minister, who was a friend of Holly's from divinity school. Plus Tim. He was my date.

After the ceremony, we all had dinner on the pier of a beachside restaurant. Nothing fancy, just fried oysters and hush puppies and corn on the cob. Holly and James brought their own champagne, and they let Tim and me each have a glass.

Everyone made a toast except for Tim. Just like you'd expect, all the toasts were about love. Some people spoke longer than others, and James's mom cried a little, saying something about how she always knew that James and Holly belonged together, and she hoped their union and the children they'd have would make the world a little brighter. I made a toast too, and thanked James for taking such good care of my hand, and said that I hoped one day I'd be as lucky as them and find my true love.

The shortest toast of the evening belonged to my mother. She stood up and raised her glass and said the very same thing that she'd said to me all those years ago, when we'd seen those two men holding hands in an elevator.

"Love is love," my mom said, raising her glass. "We smile when we see it."

I suppose you're wondering why I skipped so far ahead in time. Maybe you want to know what happened with Tim and his family, not to mention Allie and me. If you're a particularly optimistic person, you might even be hoping something came along at the last minute to save our farm.

But that would be a different story. Not mine. Not my family's. Not Tim's. It'd probably take a whole nother book to explain the step-by-step of what went on with Tim and his family. I guess it's still a work in progress. Tim's father ended up refusing to talk to the Lutheran minister that Kathy found. But his mother went. The meeting was pretty good, but Tim still wanted to stay with us. When his mom dropped him off, she and Kathy came on in to talk to my parents. The four of them sat down and drank a bottle of wine together, and Mrs. Greenlaw cried a little. My mom wouldn't tell me everything that was said, but the overall gist was that Tim was Mrs. Greenlaw's baby. When it really got down to it, no amount of religion in the world was going to stand between him and her.

Unfortunately, Tim's dad had a harder time coming around to this way of thinking. So you know what Mrs. Greenlaw finally said to him? She said, "If you think I'm going to choose you over my own child when I wouldn't even choose God, you've got another think coming." Mr. Greenlaw moved out, at least for the time being. And as it happened, Mrs. Greenlaw didn't need to give up God. She didn't even need to switch denominations. She just moved on over to the new Lutheran church, and Tim moved back in with her. He even goes with her to church on Sundays.

There were days in that second semester at Williamsport High when I sure wished Tim and I had gone back to Cutty River with Allie and Jesse. Days when Devon would make a snide remark to me (he seemed to generally ignore Tim, which I guess was bad enough considering they used to be friends), or someone would slip a nasty note into Tim's locker. Tim had to get a new cell phone number because he kept getting crank calls, and he shut down his Facebook account.

Most days, though, people left us pretty much alone. Probably they were a little confused because Tim and I were still best friends, which to the outside world looked exactly the same as boyfriend and girlfriend. We both got parts in the spring production of *A Midsummer Night's Dream*. Tim played Lysander, which is the lead romantic role. Caroline Jones played Hermia, another big romantic role, and I played a fairy named Peaseblossom, which is pretty much the smallest role in the entire play. But it was fun to be back with the old gang for afternoon rehearsals, and those are the moments that I think I will miss when I happen to look back on my last year in North Carolina. This time, as you might imagine, Caroline Jones did not host the cast party. It was at somebody else's house, and pretty much as many people got drunk as at Caroline's, just not the same people.

For a while there was talk of Tim enrolling at Hillsdale and coming north with us. In the end it was Tim who ended up saying no to that. He told his mother he would miss her too much, and that he wanted to stand his ground at Williamsport. I happen to know the real reason is that he and Jay have been meeting for walks and occasional breakfasts on the weekends—when Tim is supposedly going for walks or having breakfast with me. If you think this doesn't make me jealous, you are positively wrong.

Like the world, I still have a good deal of growing up to do.

By mid-June school let out, and most everything in our house was gone. Here's what we ended up keeping: Mom and Dad's wedding china, family pictures, most of our clothes, plus Dad's bird books, telescope, and binoculars, and Mom's and my saddles. We kept the laptop computer. We kept the station wagon but sold the Jeep. Pretty much everything else—the desktop computer, every stick of furniture and appliance and lamp and pots and pans and you better believe Dad's rifles—we sold or donated. It almost got so I couldn't wait to move; it felt like living in a ghost town. No matter which room I walked into, all I could think of was what used to be there. The last horses had been placed, and Pandora was already on her way up north. A Thoroughbred retirement center in New Hampshire had taken Sombrero, and they'd offered to give Pandora a ride up with him. The person who'd taken Sombrero was such a nice man that he said he wouldn't make Sombrero available for adoption for at least a year, so that if we got back on our feet, Mom could adopt him back. In the meantime he'd be close enough so that she could go and visit and even ride him. Mom said that center had almost closed too, so he understood how she felt. One good thing about going down the tubes at the same time as so many other people: You find a lot of sympathy.

With all the horses gone, there was pretty much nothing to do at my house, so nearly every day Allie, Jesse, Ginny, and I met Tim at the Cutty River Landing swimming pool. Sometimes Caroline and Tyler would come by, but mostly it was the five of us, and we all got along so well it seemed even more a shame that we wouldn't be at the same school next year. What really drove me crazy was all the time we'd wasted. If Tim hadn't had to worry about keeping himself a secret, the whole misunderstanding between Allie and me would have been cleared up in an instant. It's amazing how much trouble gets caused just by people not wanting to mind their own business. No matter how many times I go through it in my brain, I can't think why anyone else in the world should care whether Tim Greenlaw likes guys or girls. If the one person in the world who happens to have a legitimate gripe about it— me!—is willing to accept him for who he is, then what's your problem? Not that you have a problem. At least, I hope you don't, not after everything I've just told you.

The other day I saw a picture on the Internet of a man at a rally for marriage equality. He was holding up a sign that said, IF GOD HATES GAYS, WHY ARE WE SO CUTE? I printed it out and gave it to Tim. He showed it to his mother, and you know what she did? She hung it up on the refrigerator. Now that's what I call progress.

So finally it loomed right in front of us, July 2, the day we'd leave North Carolina for good. On top of everything else it would be the first birthday that I could remember not spending with Allie. She and I decided to have a last celebration a little early. We batted around different things to do, like having a small party, or maybe camping at the Old Farthing Road, but that didn't seem much fun without horses. So in the end we just planned on going out to dinner and then sleeping over at her house. I drove to the restaurant myself, all the way from Leeville.

Allie sat waiting for me at a table by the window. She had a little wrapped box with a bow on the plate in front of her. Even though we were celebrating my birthday, I'd brought a present for her, too, and I fished it out of my bag as soon as I sat down.

"You first," I said, as she handed me my present, and she went ahead and opened it. It was an antique frame I got at a special shop. "I thought you could frame your first picture in it," I explained. "You know, from a magazine."

"Hey, you have great timing," Allie said, beaming. Then she smiled even wider. "Because guess what? I have a job!" She told me she was going to be photographed in a local tourist brochure for Wilbur Beach. "If the pictures are good, I might even be on the cover," she said.

Wow! "That's amazing," I said. "You have to promise you won't forget me once you're a supermodel."

"If you promise not to forget me once you're a Yankee, and a famous Broadway singer. Here," she said, moving the little box to my plate. "Open mine."

In the box was little silver necklace with a pendant that looked like a heart that had been ripped in half. She'd had it engraved with her name, Allie, in pretty script. When I looked back at her, she grabbed the necklace she was wearing and held up the pendant. It was the other half of the heart, and it was engraved with the name Wren.

My eyes filled up with tears, and as soon as they did, so did hers. She reached across the table for my hand, and I gave it to her. "Oh, Wren," she said. "I'm so sad you're moving away just when things are getting right between us. I'm so sorry about everything."

I almost said, *It's okay*, then remembered that I hadn't been the best friend in the world either, and the better thing to say was, "I'm sorry too." And I *was* sorry, for the time we'd lost, and that we wouldn't see each other again till who knew when. But mostly I just felt glad, and relieved, that the two of us were friends again.

By our last night in North Carolina I had said good-bye to everyone who needed saying good-bye to. Holly and Tim both came to spend the night, to say good-bye to the farm and to us. Dad went out to get barbecue from Casey's. Before he got back with the food, Tim and I walked through the house with Holly. Now that the place wouldn't belong to us anymore, Holly could take this one evening to remember the things she loved about it. "Mama used to sew in here," she said, standing in the empty room that used to be Dad's study. "She made my prom dress, do you believe that? I went to prom in a homemade dress, like a real country girl."

Tim and I left her to say good-bye to her old room— which would soon also be my old room—by herself, and went out to join Mom and Dad at the picnic table. After a bit Holly came down too, her eyes red like she'd been crying. By now Mom and I had cried so much for this place that our eyes were finally dry. Dad had just come back with the food, and we sat around the picnic table and ate it off paper plates, with plastic sporks and knives.

We stayed out there, talking and eating, until the sun went down. Then Dad went inside and came back with an old Mason jar. He knelt down and started digging dirt with his hands and pouring it into the jar. When it was half-full, he sealed it up and gave it to me.

"I'm at peace leaving this place behind," he said. "But Wren, I think you ought to take this bit of it with you."

I could feel Daisy's tail, thumping across my feet. That familiar home-smell of Confederate jasmine wafted through the air. I didn't look at the jar with the dirt in it. Instead I turned around and looked out over the fields, which used to have cotton and rice but as long as I lived here had only been used to graze horses. I looked past the magnolia and trumpet tulip trees, to where the river ran under a canopy of moss and vine. I thought of all the times I had walked or ridden up and down our dusty driveway. It seemed to me that I had done all the thinking I could stand doing about what had happened here, so many years before I was born. Losing this land, plus all the deep sorriness in my heart, was all the penance I could bear to pay. At least for right now.

"Thanks, Dad," I said. "But I don't think I need to take this dirt. I have enough under my fingernails to last me my whole life." I pushed the jar back across the table. He looked at me a long minute, and then he opened up the jar and spilled it on top of the grass beside him.

"Okay, Wrenny," he said. "Okay."

Mom stood up and started sweeping all the paper plates

into a garbage bag. We had to eat everything, because there was no place to keep it—my parents had gone and sold the refrigerator. I'm not sure if the new owners knew how much they'd be starting from scratch out here. When I stood up, my belly was so full that I thought I might have to sit directly back down. But Tim said, "Do y'all mind if Wren and I take a walk?"

"No," Dad said. "Bring Daisy with you." As if we had a choice! The second we headed down the road, Daisy bounded after us, her collar jingling.

The night felt hot and close and muggy. Mosquitoes buzzed around our heads, and the crickets and southern toads were whooping away the night like it was some giant party. Tim grabbed my elbow and steered me toward a little clearing beside the river. The two of us sat down together on a wide tree stump.

"Have you ever been to New Hampshire before?" Tim asked.

"No. New York is the farthest north I've been."

"Washington, DC, for me."

"I've seen pictures of the school, though," I said. "Lots of pine trees. I guess there's no jasmine, though." It was hard not to think of this last fragrance, since it bloomed all around us, rising into the air with the sounds.

"There'll be other things," Tim said.

"Maybe you can visit me there."

"And you can come back here." He put his arm around me, and we stared out at the river, not saying what we knew was the truth of it—that two teenagers probably wouldn't be doing a whole lot of traveling on their own. I thought about telling Tim how much I was going to miss him next year, and how glad I was for his friendship, and maybe even that I loved him. I thought about saying, *Tim, you were my first love, and right now you're my only love, and I'll never be sorry.*

But I didn't, because just then I saw on the river what I'd thought was a log, floating near the top, and a pair of eyes, peering out of the water, watching us.

"Tim," I whispered, pointing.

He squinted through the semidarkness, and I heard a little intake of breath. "Dang!"

Without saying anything, we managed to agree on what to do, which was jump off that stump and tear back up to the house. We'd barely gone fifty feet before we started laughing, which got Daisy barking. So that's how we got back to the house, nearly doubled over and panting from running and laughing like two nutcases, while Daisy ran in mad, barking circles all around us.

Mom, Dad, and Holly spilled out of the house in a ribbon of light.

"What, Wren?" Mom said, grabbing onto me. "What on earth?"

"The alligator's back," I said, gasping, laughing.

It's hard to explain, exactly, why I felt so happy. But I broke away from my mom and fell into Tim's arms. He held me tight while I laughed against his shoulder, the two of us holding on for dear life, not thinking about how we'd have to let go in the morning, just glad to have each other right now.

Tim's arms felt old-Tim strong. I pulled back, away from him, staring into his freckly face, drinking in the smiley happiness that had started to return to it. I looked at that face, Tim's face, and I thought how I loved him. Then I let myself be honest, for a moment, about how I wanted the world to be.

I wanted my family to keep our farm, and all our horses, and never have to say good-bye to Leeville. In this dream-world, Tim would not be gay. He would be my boyfriend, the best boyfriend in the whole world, staring back at me with all the desire I had in myself for him.

But seeing as the world was not that way, I saw something else in Tim's face. And it made me stand a little taller. Because maybe nothing would ever be exactly the way I wanted it. But if Tim had the courage to stay here, in this imperfect place, then the least I could do was have the courage to leave it.

"I love you, Tim," I said.

"I love you, too, Wren."

And you don't need me to tell you that *I love you, too* is never quite the same as *I love you*. But that was all I had, so I took it. Along with everything else I'd learned from him, to face the unknown future, waiting just a day away.

* * *

nina de gramont

is the author of teen novels *Meet Me at the River* and
Every Little Thing in the World, as well as the story
collection *Of Cats and Men* and the adult novel *Gossip
of the Starlings*. Her work has appeared in *Redbook*,
Harvard Review, *Nerve*, and *Seventeen*. Nina lives with
her husband and daughter in coastal North Carolina.

You can visit her at ninadegramont.com.